# HYPNOS

# HYPNOS

Volume 8, Issue 2

Edited by

Dylan Henderson
Breanna Pearl,
Evan Eugene,
&
Kristen Marie

Hypnos Magazine – Radium Town, OK

Published in the United States by Hypnos Magazine,
702 N. Dorothy Ave., Radium Town, OK 74017

www.hypnosmagazine.com

Printed in the United States
Cover design: Dylan Henderson
Cover illustration: Rick Guidice
Text design: Kester Dye
10 9 8 7 6 5 4 3 2 1

# TABLE OF CONTENTS

THE REPLACEMENT. . . . . . . . . . . . . . .Lawrence Barksdale   7

RIVAL GHOSTS. . . . . . . . . . . . . . . . . . . Brander Matthews   15

THE NIGHT AT THE HOGG. . . . . . . . . . . . . . .Bill Wright   37

MRS. DAVENPORT'S GHOST . . . . . . Frederick P. Schrader   49

THE GIVERS. . . . . . . . . . . . . . . . . . . . . . . . . .John S. Price   57

COMPENSATION. . . . . . . . . . . . . . . . . . . .Charles V. Tench   67

RED CHURCH. . . . . . . . . . . . . . . . . . . . . Dylan Henderson   85

# THE REPLACEMENT

by Lawrence Barksdale

T HE CLERK LOOKED ANNOYED. A BEAD OF SWEAT had gathered near the top of her forehead, just below her blonde hair. Irritated, she wiped it away with the back of her hand.

"Look, Mr. Roth, there's nothing I can do. You'll have to make the best of the situation. In thirty days, you can appeal the decision. That's all I can say."

The room seemed to be vibrating slightly, as if an earthquake, unnoticed by everyone else, were shaking the building.

"I can't," I said, steadying myself on the desk, "wait thirty days. They won't allow me into my office. They won't allow me access to my computer, my things.... I can't.... I can't wait thirty days. You understand that, right?"

The clerk sighed and, pushing her chair back, turned to look at me. The air conditioner in the building wasn't working, and her cheeks, neck, and chest had turned a blotchy red.

"If you want, you can fill out an application for any private property you have in your office. There's a form in the lobby, next to the water fountain. I don't know what else to tell you."

The anger inside of me was building, but I knew I had to control it.

"Tonight," I said slowly, "it'll come home, right? It'll come to our house."

The girl frowned. There was no trace of sympathy on her face.

"Technically, Mr. Roth, it's *his* house. He has every right to be there."

"*His* house?" I said, trying to remain calm.

"Yes, Mr. Roth, he has a gender, just like you do. And, according to the law, he owns the house and everything in it."

I started to interrupt, but the girl, her voice rising, ignored me.

"You will *have* to make the best of it, Mr. Roth. You do not have any choice in the matter. After thirty days, you can appeal the committee's decision. That's all you can do."

I sat back in my chair. The room had stopped shaking. Everything had become strangely still—and oddly quiet. I could no longer hear the other clerks talking on the phone or typing on their computers. Even the noisy metal fan the girl had put on the edge of her desk had become inaudible. The only thing I could hear—or feel—was a deep, rhythmic pounding between my ears.

When the girl spoke again, her voice had softened.

"Go home, Mr. Roth. Try to think of this as a vacation. I mean, you don't have to work anymore, do you? Just try to enjoy your life. Who knows? Maybe the committee will reverse its decision. That happens, you know—every now and then."

"Can.... Can I still go home?" I asked. "I mean, they didn't change the locks, did they? I'm still allowed to live there?"

The clerk laughed, her teeth sparkling behind her lipstick.

"Of course, you are," she said cheerily. "Now, go home, Mr. Roth. It's almost four. You'll want to prepare your wife for this evening."

"I will," I said, standing up.

I felt as if I were underwater. A barrier of some sort seemed to exist between me and the world around me. I moved through it as if I had been stunned.

"Mr. Roth? Just remember, if you try to hurt him—in any way—there will be legal repercussions. You have enough problems right now. You don't want to add to them."

She took a sheaf of papers, stapled them, and then pushed them across the table.

"Have a good day," she said and, without waiting for a response, turned back to her computer.

Without really understanding what I was doing, I picked up the papers and, tucking them under my arm, turned to leave. I was, according to the law, no longer a person.

"He's taller than you," my wife said, a hint of mockery in her voice, "by at least an inch."

"It doesn't look like me at all," I said, sitting down at the kitchen table.

"Peter, please, he could be your twin. He looks more like you than you do. Of course, he's not as fat."

I didn't respond. When I told her the news, she had been less upset than I expected. Truthfully, she didn't seem upset at all. She had warned me—for months—that this might happen, that I might go too far. Now the thing was here, and she didn't seem to mind. Well, why should she? Our relationship had soured a long time ago.

"What's it doing?" I asked, picking up a leftover piece of toast. "Aren't you curious?"

Aubrey switched off the water and, turning around, leaned against the kitchen sink.

"He's reading a book, Peter, okay? That's all."

"Why?" I asked, staring down the hallway at the bedroom door. "Does it really enjoy reading, or is it just pretending to read—for our benefit?"

"Oh, leave him alone. You're making it worse, Peter. Why do you have to make everything so complicated?"

I looked at her. She was, even after all these years, still pretty, but there was a maliciousness in her—a hatefulness. She seemed to be enjoying my misery.

"How ... am I making things complicated, Aubrey? I've ... lost *everything*. I don't even have a Social Security number. I can't.... I can't even apply for a credit card."

"You can have that chair," Aubrey snapped. "You can have a place at the table. We'll feed you. You can sleep on the couch or put a bed in the alcove—where the highboy is. What more do you want, Peter? You're not working. You're not earning anything."

I could feel my anger rising.

"I *paid* for this house," I said, my teeth clenched. "I bought it. I own it. That ... thing doesn't have any right to be here!"

Aubrey didn't say anything. Then, with a sigh, she turned back to the sink and began scrubbing dishes.

"It is your house, Peter. Nobody's taken it away from you. You're enjoying it right now—while you read your book in the bedroom."

That night I slept in the hallway, just outside the bedroom door. They didn't try to hide their lovemaking from me: I could hear them through the wall. He was, I quickly realized, a much better lover than I was—or ever had been. I listened to them for a long time, and then gathering my blankets and pillow together, I staggered to the back porch. It was a warm night and humid, but just as the sun was coming up, I fell into a heavy sleep that lasted until well into the afternoon. When I finally awoke, my head throbbing, I saw the thing, its face wonderfully smooth, standing over me.

"What do you want?" I asked, wiping the sweat from my face and forehead. "Why don't you get away from me?"

The thing, smiling faintly, crouched down and began to rock back and forth on its mechanical heels.

"You can't be sleeping outside," it said. "Your neighbors don't want to look out their window and see a man sleeping on his back porch."

"Where do you suggest I sleep?" I said, struggling to rise. "Where do you want me to go?"

"There are places."

A chill ran down my spine. I shivered all over.

"I'm not going there. I haven't done anything."

The thing wasn't looking at me. It was staring at the backyard, as if deep in thought.

"Maybe you haven't done anything; maybe you've done too much. It doesn't really matter, though, does it? You're not fit. You're.... You're not fit for this ... this life."

I was having trouble breathing. A part of me wondered if I were losing my mind. This couldn't be happening.

"It's happened to others. It happened to Will Doyle, didn't it? It happened to Rob Lynch."

"They deserved it," I hissed. "They said Will choked that little boy. They said he beat him and his sister."

The thing nodded.

"That's true. What about Robert?"

"He was always strange. Everyone knew ... he wasn't ... right in the head."

The thing whistled.

"That's quite a phrase, isn't it? There are so many ways someone could be not quite 'right in the head.'"

"If I hit you," I said suddenly, my fingers gripping the railing that ran around the porch, "would you even feel it?"

The thing looked at me, its glass eyes twinkling.

"I would be aware of it."

"But you wouldn't … *hurt*, would you?"

"No."

I swallowed. I was talking to myself in a mirror.

"When you were sleeping with my wife last night, you didn't feel anything, did you? You were just … aware."

The thing smiled.

"I don't need to feel anything. She felt something. That's all that really matters, isn't it?"

"Is it?" I asked, my voice filled with bitterness. "Maybe I want to feel something, too. Maybe I don't want to be like you. Maybe I want to feel."

"Maybe you feel too much."

I sat down on the porch steps. The conversation had exhausted me. Looking at the thing was exhausting.

"My son," I said after a moment's pause. "You won't stay away from him, will you?"

The thing sat down beside me and, bending forward, snapped off a dandelion. It twirled the weed for a moment, its eyes following the movement closely, as if the thing had never seen anything so marvelous. Then Peter turned to me and smiled.

"Would I be a very good father if I did that?"

A feeling, a weight, had settled at the bottom of my stomach. I felt sick.

"You would think they would know," I murmured. "That's the funny part. That's the really funny part. You would think that they would know. You're not really like me—not really."

Peter Roth grinned and, tossing the weed into the bushes, rose. "They know."

# THE RIVAL GHOSTS

by Brander Matthews

THE GOOD SHIP SPED ON HER WAY ACROSS THE calm Atlantic. It was an outward passage, according to the little charts which the company had charily distributed, but most of the passengers were homeward bound, after a summer of rest and recreation, and they were counting the days before they might hope to see Fire Island Light. On the lee side of the boat, comfortably sheltered from the wind, and just by the door of the captain's room (which was theirs during the day), sat a little group of returning Americans. The Duchess (she was down on the purser's list as Mrs. Martin, but her friends and familiars called her the Duchess of Washington Square) and Baby Van Rensselaer (she was quite old enough to vote, had her sex been entitled to that duty, but as the younger of two sisters she was still the baby of the family)—the Duchess and Baby Van Rensselaer were discussing the pleasant English voice and the not unpleasant English accent of a manly young lordling who was going to America for sport. Uncle Larry and Dear Jones were enticing each other into a bet on the ship's run of the morrow.

"I'll give you two to one she don't make 420," said Dear Jones.

"I'll take it," answered Uncle Larry. "We made 427 the fifth day last year." It was Uncle Larry's seventeenth visit to Europe, and this was therefore his thirty-fourth voyage.

"And when did you get in?" asked Baby Van Rensselaer. "I don't care a bit about the run, so long as we get in soon."

"We crossed the bar Sunday night, just seven days after we left Queenstown, and we dropped anchor off Quarantine at three o'clock on Monday morning."

"I hope we shan't do that this time. I can't seem to sleep any when the boat stops."

"I can; but I didn't," continued Uncle Larry; "because my state-room was the most for'ard in the boat, and the donkey-engine that let down the anchor was right over my head."

"So you got up and saw the sunrise over the bay," said Dear Jones, "with the electric lights of the city twinkling in the distance, and the first faint flush of the dawn in the east just over Fort Lafayette, and the rosy tinge which spread softly upward, and——"

"Did you both come back together?" asked the Duchess.

"Because he has crossed thirty-four times you must not suppose that he has a monopoly in sunrises," retorted Dear Jones. "No, this was my own sunrise; and a mighty pretty one it was, too."

"I'm not matching sunrises with you," remarked Uncle Larry, calmly; "but I'm willing to back a merry jest called forth by my sunrise against any two merry jests called forth by yours."

"I confess reluctantly that my sunrise evoked no merry jest at all." Dear Jones was an honest man, and would scorn to invent a merry jest on the spur of the moment.

"That's where my sunrise has the call," said Uncle Larry, complacently.

"What was the merry jest?" was Baby Van Rensselaer's inquiry, the natural result of a feminine curiosity thus artistically excited.

"Well, here it is. I was standing aft, near a patriotic American and a wandering Irishman, and the patriotic American rashly declared that you couldn't see a sunrise like that anywhere in Europe, and this gave the Irishman his chance, and he said, 'Sure ye don't have 'em here till we're through with 'em over there.'"

"It is true," said Dear Jones, thoughtfully, "that they do have some things over there better than we do; for instance, umbrellas."

"And gowns," added the Duchess.

"And antiquities,"—this was Uncle Larry's contribution.

"And we do have some things so much better in America!" protested Baby Van Rensselaer, as yet uncorrupted by any worship of the effete monarchies of despotic Europe. "We make lots of things a great deal nicer than you can get them in Europe—especially ice-cream."

"And pretty girls," added Dear Jones; but he did not look at her.

"And spooks," remarked Uncle Larry casually.

"Spooks?" queried the Duchess.

"Spooks. I maintain the word. Ghosts, if you like that better, or specters. We turn out the best quality of spook——"

"You forget the lovely ghost stories about the Rhine, and the Black Forest," interrupted Miss Van Rensselaer, with feminine inconsistency.

"I remember the Rhine and the Black Forest and all the other haunts of elves and fairies and hobgoblins; but for good honest spooks there is no place like home. And what differentiates our spook—*Spiritus Americanus*—from the ordinary ghost of literature is that it responds to the American sense of humor.

17

Take Irving's stories for example. *The Headless Horseman*, that's a comic ghost story. And Rip Van Winkle—consider what humor, and what good-humor, there is in the telling of his meeting with the goblin crew of Hendrik Hudson's men! A still better example of this American way of dealing with legend and mystery is the marvelous tale of the rival ghosts."

"The rival ghosts?" queried the Duchess and Baby Van Rensselaer together. "Who were they?"

"Didn't I ever tell you about them?" answered Uncle Larry, a gleam of approaching joy flashing from his eye.

"Since he is bound to tell us sooner or later, we'd better be resigned and hear it now," said Dear Jones.

"If you are not more eager, I won't tell it at all."

"Oh, do, Uncle Larry; you know I just dote on ghost stories," pleaded Baby Van Rensselaer.

"Once upon a time," began Uncle Larry—"in fact, a very few years ago—there lived in the thriving town of New York a young American called Duncan—Eliphalet Duncan. Like his name, he was half Yankee and half Scotch, and naturally he was a lawyer, and had come to New York to make his way. His father was a Scotchman, who had come over and settled in Boston, and married a Salem girl. When Eliphalet Duncan was about twenty he lost both of his parents. His father left him with enough money to give him a start, and a strong feeling of pride in his Scotch birth; you see there was a title in the family in Scotland, and although Eliphalet's father was the younger son of a younger son, yet he always remembered, and always bade his only son to remember, that his ancestry was noble. His mother left him her full share of Yankee grit, and a little house in Salem which has belonged to her family for more than two hundred years. She was a Hitchcock, and the Hitchcocks had been settled in Salem since the year 1. It was a great-great-grandfather of Mr.

Eliphalet Hitchcock who was foremost in the time of the Salem witchcraft craze. And this little old house which she left to my friend Eliphalet Duncan was haunted.

"By the ghost of one of the witches, of course," interrupted Dear Jones.

"Now how could it be the ghost of a witch, since the witches were all burned at the stake? You never heard of anybody who was burned having a ghost, did you?"

"That's an argument in favor of cremation, at any rate," replied Jones, evading the direct question.

"It is, if you don't like ghosts; I do," said Baby Van Rensselaer.

"And so do I," added Uncle Larry. "I love a ghost as dearly as an Englishman loves a lord."

"Go on with your story," said the Duchess, majestically overruling all extraneous discussion.

"This little old house at Salem was haunted," resumed Uncle Larry. "And by a very distinguished ghost—or at least by a ghost with very remarkable attributes."

"What was he like?" asked Baby Van Rensselaer, with a premonitory shiver of anticipatory delight.

"It had a lot of peculiarities. In the first place, it never appeared to the master of the house. Mostly it confined its visitations to unwelcome guests. In the course of the last hundred years it had frightened away four successive mothers-in-law, while never intruding on the head of the household."

"I guess that ghost had been one of the boys when he was alive and in the flesh." This was Dear Jones's contribution to the telling of the tale.

"In the second place," continued Uncle Larry, "it never frightened anybody the first time it appeared. Only on the second visit were the ghost-seers scared; but then they were scared enough for twice, and they rarely mustered up courage enough to risk a third interview. One of the most curious characteristics of this well-meaning spook was that it had no face—or at least that nobody ever saw its face."

"Perhaps he kept his countenance veiled?" queried the Duchess, who was beginning to remember that she never did like ghost stories.

"That was what I was never able to find out. I have asked several people who saw the ghost, and none of them could tell me anything about its face, and yet while in its presence they never noticed its features, and never remarked on their absence or concealment. It was only afterward when they tried to recall calmly all the circumstances of meeting with the mysterious stranger, that they became aware that they had not seen its face. And they could not say whether the features were covered, or whether they were wanting, or what the trouble was. They knew only that the face was never seen. And no matter how often they might see it, they never fathomed this mystery. To this day nobody knows whether the ghost which used to haunt the little old house in Salem had a face, or what manner of face it had."

"How awfully weird!" said Baby Van Rensselaer. "And why did the ghost go away?"

"I haven't said it went away," answered Uncle Larry, with much dignity.

"But you said it *used* to haunt the little old house at Salem, so I supposed it had moved. Didn't it?"

"You shall be told in due time. Eliphalet Duncan used to spend most of his summer vacations at Salem, and the ghost never bothered him at all, for he was the master of the house— much to his disgust, too, because he wanted to see for himself the mysterious tenant at will of his property. But he never saw it, never. He arranged with friends to call him whenever it might appear, and he slept in the next room with the door open; and yet when their frightened cries waked him the ghost was gone, and his only reward was to hear reproachful sighs as soon as he went back to bed. You see, the ghost thought it was not fair of Eliphalet to seek an introduction which was plainly unwelcome."

Dear Jones interrupted the story-teller by getting up and tucking a heavy rug snugly around Baby Van Rensselaer's feet, for the sky was now overcast and gray, and the air was damp and penetrating.

"One fine spring morning," pursued Uncle Larry, "Eliphalet Duncan received great news. I told you that there was a title in the family in Scotland, and that Eliphalet's father was the younger son of a younger son. Well, it happened that all Eliphalet's father's brothers and uncles had died off without male issue except the eldest son of the eldest, and he, of course, bore the title, and was Baron Duncan of Duncan. Now the great news that Eliphalet Duncan received in New York one fine spring morning was that Baron Duncan and his only son had been yachting in the Hebrides, and they had been caught in a black squall, and they were both dead. So my friend Eliphalet Duncan inherited the title and the estates."

"How romantic!" said the Duchess. "So he was a baron!"

"Well," answered Uncle Larry, "he was a baron if he chose. But he didn't choose."

"More fool he," said Dear Jones sententiously.

"Well," answered Uncle Larry, "I'm not so sure of that. You see, Eliphalet Duncan was half Scotch and half Yankee, and he had two eyes to the main chance. He held his tongue about his windfall of luck until he could find out whether the Scotch estates were enough to keep up the Scotch title. He soon discovered that they were not, and that the late Lord Duncan, having married money, kept up such state as he could out of the revenues of the dowry of Lady Duncan. And Eliphalet, he decided that he would rather be a well-fed lawyer in New York, living comfortably on his practice, than a starving lord in Scotland, living scantily on his title."

"But he kept his title?" asked the Duchess.

"Well," answered Uncle Larry, "he kept it quiet. I knew it, and a friend or two more. But Eliphalet was a sight too smart to put Baron Duncan of Duncan, Attorney and Counselor at Law, on his shingle."

"What has all this got to do with your ghost?" asked Dear Jones pertinently.

"Nothing with that ghost, but a good deal with another ghost. Eliphalet was very learned in spirit lore—perhaps because he owned the haunted house at Salem, perhaps because he was a Scotchman by descent. At all events, he had made a special study of the wraiths and white ladies and banshees and bogies of all kinds whose sayings and doings and warnings are recorded in the annals of the Scottish nobility. In fact, he was acquainted with the habits of every reputable spook in the Scotch peerage. And he knew that there was a Duncan ghost attached to the person of the holder of the title of Baron Duncan of Duncan."

"So, besides being the owner of a haunted house in Salem, he was also a haunted man in Scotland?" asked Baby Van Rensselaer.

"Just so. But the Scotch ghost was not unpleasant, like the Salem ghost, although it had one peculiarity in common with its trans-Atlantic fellow-spook. It never appeared to the holder of the title, just as the other never was visible to the owner of the house. In fact, the Duncan ghost was never seen at all. It was a guardian angel only. Its sole duty was to be in personal attendance on Baron Duncan of Duncan, and to warn him of impending evil. The traditions of the house told that the Barons of Duncan had again and again felt a premonition of ill fortune. Some of them had yielded and withdrawn from the venture they had undertaken, and it had failed dismally. Some had been obstinate, and had hardened their hearts, and had gone on reckless of defeat and to death. In no case had a Lord Duncan been exposed to peril without fair warning."

"Then how came it that the father and son were lost in the yacht off the Hebrides?" asked Dear Jones.

"Because they were too enlightened to yield to superstition. There is extant now a letter of Lord Duncan, written to his wife a few minutes before he and his son set sail, in which he tells her how hard he has had to struggle with an almost overmastering desire to give up the trip. Had he obeyed the friendly warning of the family ghost, the latter would have been spared a journey across the Atlantic."

"Did the ghost leave Scotland for America as soon as the old baron died?" asked Baby Van Rensselaer, with much interest.

"How did he come over," queried Dear Jones—"in the steerage, or as a cabin passenger?"

"I don't know," answered Uncle Larry calmly, "and Eliphalet, he didn't know. For as he was in no danger, and stood in no need of warning, he couldn't tell whether the ghost was on duty or not. Of course he was on the watch for it all the time. But he never got any proof of its presence until he went down to the little old house of Salem, just before the Fourth of July. He took a friend down with him—a young fellow who had been in the regular army since the day Fort Sumter was fired on, and who thought that after four years of the little unpleasantness down South, including six months in Libby, and after ten years of fighting the bad Indians on the plains, he wasn't likely to be much frightened by a ghost. Well, Eliphalet and the officer sat out on the porch all the evening smoking and talking over points in military law. A little after twelve o'clock, just as they began to think it was about time to turn in, they heard the most ghastly noise in the house. It wasn't a shriek, or a howl, or a yell, or anything they could put a name to. It was an undeterminate, inexplicable shiver and shudder of sound, which went wailing out of the window. The officer had been at Cold Harbor, but he felt himself getting colder this time. Eliphalet knew it was the ghost who haunted the house. As this weird sound died away, it was followed by another, sharp, short, blood-curdling in its intensity. Something in this cry seemed familiar to Eliphalet, and he felt sure that it proceeded from the family ghost, the warning wraith of the Duncans."

"Do I understand you to intimate that both ghosts were there together?" inquired the Duchess anxiously.

"Both of them were there," answered Uncle Larry. "You see, one of them belonged to the house, and had to be there all the time, and the other was attached to the person of Baron Duncan, and had to follow him there; wherever he was there was the ghost also. But Eliphalet, he had scarcely time to think this out when he heard both sounds again, not one after another, but both together, and something told him—some sort of an instinct he had—that those two ghosts didn't agree, didn't get on together, didn't exactly hit it off; in fact, that they were quarreling."

"Quarreling ghosts! Well, I never!" was Baby Van Rensselaer's remark.

"It is a blessed thing to see ghosts dwell together in unity," said Dear Jones.

And the Duchess added, "It would certainly be setting a better example."

"You know," resumed Uncle Larry, "that two waves of light or of sound may interfere and produce darkness or silence. So it was with these rival spooks. They interfered, but they did not produce silence or darkness. On the contrary, as soon as Eliphalet and the officer went into the house, there began at once a series of spiritualistic manifestations, a regular dark séance. A tambourine was played upon, a bell was rung, and a flaming banjo went singing around the room."

"Where did they get the banjo?" asked Dear Jones skeptically.

"I don't know. Materialized it, maybe, just as they did the tambourine. You don't suppose a quiet New York lawyer kept a stock of musical instruments large enough to fit out a strolling minstrel troupe just on the chance of a pair of ghosts coming to give him a surprise party, do you? Every spook has its own instrument of torture. Angels play on harps, I'm informed, and spirits delight in banjos and tambourines. These spooks of Eliphalet Duncan's were ghosts with all the modern improvements, and I guess they were capable of providing their own musical weapons. At all events, they had them there in the little old house at Salem the night Eliphalet and his friend came down. And they played on them, and they rang the bell, and they rapped here, there, and everywhere. And they kept it up all night."

"All night?" asked the awe-stricken Duchess.

"All night long," said Uncle Larry solemnly; "and the next night, too. Eliphalet did not get a wink of sleep, neither did his friend. On the second night the house ghost was seen by the officer; on the third night it showed itself again; and the next morning the officer packed his grip-sack and took the first train to Boston. He was a New Yorker, but he said he'd sooner go to Boston than see that ghost again. Eliphalet, he wasn't scared at all, partly because he never saw either the domiciliary or the titular spook, and partly because he felt himself on friendly terms with the spirit world, and didn't scare easily. But after losing three nights' sleep and the society of his friend, he began to be a little impatient, and to think that the thing had gone far enough. You see, while in a way he was fond of ghosts, yet he liked them best one at a time. Two ghosts were one too many. He wasn't bent on making a collection of spooks. He and one ghost were company, but he and two ghosts were a crowd."

"What did he do?" asked Baby Van Rensselaer.

"Well, he couldn't do anything. He waited awhile, hoping they would get tired; but he got tired out first. You see, it comes natural to a spook to sleep in the daytime, but a man wants to sleep nights, and they wouldn't let him sleep nights. They kept on wrangling and quarreling incessantly; they manifested and they dark-séanced as regularly as the old clock on the stairs struck twelve; they rapped and they rang bells and they banged the tambourine and they threw the flaming banjo about the house, and worse than all, they swore."

"I did not know that spirits were addicted to bad language," said the Duchess.

"How did he know they were swearing? Could he hear them?" asked Dear Jones.

"That was just it," responded Uncle Larry; "he could not hear them—at least not distinctly. There were inarticulate murmurs and stifled rumblings. But the impression produced on him was that they were swearing. If they had only sworn right out, he would not have minded it so much, because he would have known the worst. But the feeling that the air was full of suppressed profanity was very wearing and after standing it for a week, he gave up in disgust and went to the White Mountains."

"Leaving them to fight it out, I suppose," interjected Baby Van Rensselaer.

"Not at all," explained Uncle Larry. "They could not quarrel unless he was present. You see, he could not leave the titular ghost behind him, and the domiciliary ghost could not leave the house. When he went away he took the family ghost with him, leaving the house ghost behind. Now spooks can't quarrel when they are a hundred miles apart any more than men can."

"And what happened afterward?" asked Baby Van Rensselaer, with a pretty impatience.

"A most marvelous thing happened. Eliphalet Duncan went to the White Mountains, and in the car of the railroad that runs to the top of Mount Washington he met a classmate whom he had not seen for years, and this classmate introduced Duncan to his sister, and this sister was a remarkably pretty girl, and Duncan fell in love with her at first sight, and by the time he got to the top of Mount Washington he was so deep in love that he began to consider his own unworthiness, and to wonder whether she might ever be induced to care for him a little—ever so little."

"I don't think that is so marvelous a thing," said Dear Jones glancing at Baby Van Rensselaer.

"Who was she?" asked the Duchess, who had once lived in Philadelphia.

"She was Miss Kitty Sutton, of San Francisco, and she was a daughter of old Judge Sutton, of the firm of Pixley and Sutton."

"A very respectable family," assented the Duchess.

"I hope she wasn't a daughter of that loud and vulgar old Mrs. Sutton whom I met at Saratoga, one summer, four or five years ago?" said Dear Jones.

"Probably she was."

"She was a horrid old woman. The boys used to call her Mother Gorgon."

"The pretty Kitty Sutton with whom Eliphalet Duncan had fallen in love was the daughter of Mother Gorgon. But he never saw the mother, who was in 'Frisco, or Los Angeles, or Santa Fe, or somewhere out West, and he saw a great deal of the daughter, who was up in the White Mountains. She was traveling with her brother and his wife, and as they journeyed from hotel to hotel, Duncan went with them, and filled out the quartette. Before the end of the summer he began to think about proposing. Of course he had lots of chances, going on excursions as they were every day. He made up his mind to seize the first opportunity, and that very evening he took her out for a moonlight row on Lake Winnipiseogee. As he handed her into the boat he resolved to do it, and he had a glimmer of a suspicion that she knew he was going to do it, too."

"Girls," said Dear Jones, "never go out in a rowboat at night with a young man unless you mean to accept him."

"Sometimes it's best to refuse him, and get it over once for all," said Baby Van Rensselaer.

"As Eliphalet took the oars he felt a sudden chill. He tried to shake it off, but in vain. He began to have a growing consciousness of impending evil. Before he had taken ten strokes—and he was a swift oarsman—he was aware of a mysterious presence between him and Miss Sutton."

"Was it the guardian-angel ghost warning him off the match?" interrupted Dear Jones.

"That's just what it was," said Uncle Larry. "And he yielded to it, and kept his peace, and rowed Miss Sutton back to the hotel with his proposal unspoken."

"More fool he," said Dear Jones. "It will take more than one ghost to keep me from proposing when my mind is made up." And he looked at Baby Van Rensselaer.

"The next morning," continued Uncle Larry, "Eliphalet overslept himself, and when he went down to a late breakfast he found that the Suttons had gone to New York by the morning train. He wanted to follow them at once, and again he felt the mysterious presence overpowering his will. He struggled two days, and at last he roused himself to do what he wanted in spite of the spook. When he arrived in New York it was late in the evening. He dressed himself hastily and went to the hotel where the Suttons put up, in the hope of seeing at least her brother. The guardian angel fought every inch of the walk with him, until he began to wonder whether, if Miss Sutton were to take him, the spook would forbid the banns. At the hotel he saw no one that night, and he went home determined to call as early as he could the next afternoon, and make an end of it. When he left his office about two o'clock the next day to learn his fate, he had not walked five blocks before he discovered that the wraith of the Duncans had withdrawn his opposition to the suit. There was no feeling of impending evil, no resistance, no struggle, no consciousness of an opposing presence. Eliphalet was greatly encouraged. He walked briskly to the hotel; he found Miss Sutton alone. He asked her the question, and got his answer."

"She accepted him, of course," said Baby Van Rensselaer.

"Of course," said Uncle Larry. "And while they were in the first flush of joy, swapping confidences and confessions, her brother came into the parlor with an expression of pain on his face and a telegram in his hand. The former was caused by the latter, which was from 'Frisco, and which announced the sudden death of Mrs. Sutton, their mother."

"And that was why the ghost no longer opposed the match?" questioned Dear Jones.

"Exactly. You see, the family ghost knew that Mother Gorgon was an awful obstacle to Duncan's happiness, so it warned him. But the moment the obstacle was removed, it gave its consent at once."

The fog was lowering its thick damp curtain, and it was beginning to be difficult to see from one end of the boat to the other. Dear Jones tightened the rug which enwrapped Baby Van

Rensselaer, and then withdrew again into his own substantial coverings.

Uncle Larry paused in his story long enough to light another of the tiny cigars he always smoked.

"I infer that Lord Duncan"—the Duchess was scrupulous in the bestowal of titles—"saw no more of the ghosts after he was married."

"He never saw them at all, at any time, either before or since. But they came very near breaking off the match, and thus breaking two young hearts."

"You don't mean to say that they knew any just cause or impediment why they should not forever after hold their peace?" asked Dear Jones.

"How could a ghost, or even two ghosts, keep a girl from marrying the man she loved?" This was Baby Van Rensselaer's question.

"It seems curious, doesn't it?" and Uncle Larry tried to warm himself by two or three sharp pulls at his fiery little cigar. "And the circumstances are quite as curious as the fact itself. You see, Miss Sutton wouldn't be married for a year after her mother's death, so she and Duncan had lots of time to tell each other all they knew. Eliphalet, he got to know a good deal about the girls she went to school with, and Kitty, she learned all about his family. He didn't tell her about the title for a long time, as he wasn't one to brag. But he described to her the little old house at Salem. And one evening toward the end of the summer, the wedding-day having been appointed for early in September, she told him that she didn't want to bridal tour at all; she just wanted to go down to the little old house at Salem to spend her honeymoon in peace and quiet, with nothing to do and nobody to bother them. Well, Eliphalet jumped at the suggestion. It suited him down to the ground. All of a sudden he remembered the spooks, and it knocked him all of a heap. He had told her about the Duncan Banshee, and the idea of having an ancestral ghost in personal attendance on her husband tickled her immensely. But he had never said anything about the ghost which haunted the little old house at Salem. He knew she would be frightened out of her wits if the house ghost revealed itself to her, and he saw at once that it would be impossible to go to Salem on their wedding trip. So he told her all about it, and how whenever he went to Salem the two ghosts interfered, and gave dark séances and manifested and materialized and made the place absolutely impossible. Kitty, she listened in silence, and Eliphalet, he thought she had changed her mind. But she hadn't done anything of the kind."

"Just like a man—to think she was going to," remarked Baby Van Rensselaer.

"She just told him she could not bear ghosts herself, but she would not marry a man who was afraid of them."

"Just like a girl—to be so inconsistent," remarked Dear Jones.

Uncle Larry's tiny cigar had long been extinct. He lighted a new one, and continued: "Eliphalet protested in vain. Kitty said her mind was made up. She was determined to pass her honeymoon in the little old house at Salem, and she was equally determined not to go there as long as there were any ghosts there. Until he could assure her that the spectral tenants had received notice to quit, and that there was no danger of manifestations and materializing, she refused to be married at all. She did not intend to have her honeymoon interrupted by two wrangling ghosts, and the wedding could be postponed until he had made ready the house for her."

"She was an unreasonable young woman," said the Duchess.

"Well, that's what Eliphalet thought, much as he was in love with her. And he believed he could talk her out of her determination. But he couldn't. She was set. And when a girl is set, there's nothing to do but yield to the inevitable. And that's just what Eliphalet did. He saw he would either have to give her up or to get the ghosts out; and as he loved her and did not care for the ghosts, he resolved to tackle the ghosts. He had clear grit, Eliphalet had—he was half Scotch and half Yankee, and neither breed turns tail in a hurry. So he made his plans and he went down to Salem. As he said good-by to Kitty he had an impression that she was sorry she had made him go, but she kept up bravely, and put a bold face on it, and saw him off, and went home and cried for an hour, and was perfectly miserable until he came back the next day."

"Did he succeed in driving the ghosts away?" asked Baby Van Rensselaer, with great interest.

"That's just what I'm coming to," said Uncle Larry, pausing at the critical moment, in the manner of the trained story teller. "You see, Eliphalet had got a rather tough job, and he would gladly have had an extension of time on the contract, but he had to choose between the girl and the ghosts, and he wanted the girl. He tried to invent or remember some short and easy way with ghosts, but he couldn't. He wished that somebody had invented a specific for spooks—something that would make the ghosts come out of the house and die in the yard. He wondered if he could not tempt the ghosts to run in debt, so that he might get the sheriff to help him. He wondered also whether the ghosts could not be overcome with strong drink—a dissipated spook, a spook with delirium tremens, might be committed to the inebriate asylum. But none of these things seemed feasible."

"What did he do?" interrupted Dear Jones. "The learned counsel will please speak to the point."

"You will regret this unseemly haste," said Uncle Larry, gravely, "when you know what really happened."

"What was it, Uncle Larry?" asked Baby Van Rensselaer. "I'm all impatience."

And Uncle Larry proceeded:

"Eliphalet went down to the little old house at Salem, and as soon as the clock struck twelve the rival ghosts began wrangling as before. Raps here, there, and everywhere, ringing bells, banging tambourines, strumming banjos sailing about the room, and all the other manifestations and materializations followed one another just as they had the summer before. The only difference Eliphalet could detect was a stronger flavor in the spectral profanity; and this, of course, was only a vague impression, for he did not actually hear a single word. He waited awhile in patience, listening and watching. Of course he never saw either of the ghosts, because neither of them could appear to him. At last he got his dander up, and he thought it was about time to interfere, so he rapped on the table, and asked for silence. As soon as he felt that the spooks were listening to him he explained the situation to them. He told them he was in love, and that he could not marry unless they vacated the house. He appealed to them as old friends, and he laid claim to their gratitude. The titular ghost had been sheltered by the Duncan family for hundreds of years, and the domiciliary ghost had had free lodging in the little old house at Salem for nearly two centuries. He implored them to settle their differences, and to get him out of his difficulty at once. He suggested they'd better fight it out then and there, and see who was master. He had brought down with him all needful weapons. And he pulled out his valise, and spread on the table a pair of navy revolvers, a pair of shot-guns, a pair of dueling swords, and a couple of bowie-knives. He offered to serve as second for both parties, and to give the word when to begin. He also took out of his valise a pack of cards and a bottle of poison, telling them that if they wished to avoid carnage they might cut the cards to see which one should take the poison. Then he waited anxiously for their reply. For a little space there was silence. Then he became conscious of a tremulous shivering in one corner of the room, and he remembered that he had heard from that direction what sounded like a frightened sigh when he made the first suggestion of the duel. Something told him that this was the domiciliary ghost, and that it was badly scared. Then he was impressed by a certain movement in the opposite corner of the room, as though the titular ghost were drawing himself up with offended dignity. Eliphalet couldn't exactly see these things, because he never saw the ghosts, but he felt them. After a silence of nearly a minute a voice came from the corner where the family ghost stood—a voice strong and full, but trembling slightly with suppressed passion. And this voice told Eliphalet it was plain enough that he had not long been the head of the Duncans, and that he had never properly considered the characteristics of his race if now he supposed that one of his blood could draw his sword against a woman. Eliphalet said he had never suggested that the Duncan ghost should raise his hand against a woman and all he wanted was that the Duncan ghost should fight the other ghost. And then the voice told Eliphalet that the other ghost was a woman."

"What?" said Dear Jones, sitting up suddenly. "You don't mean to tell me that the ghost which haunted the house was a woman?"

"Those were the very words Eliphalet Duncan used," said Uncle Larry; "but he did not need to wait for the answer. All at once he recalled the traditions about the domiciliary ghost, and he knew that what the titular ghost said was the fact. He had never thought of the sex of a spook, but there was no doubt whatever that the house ghost was a woman. No sooner was this

34

firmly fixed in Eliphalet's mind than he saw his way out of the difficulty. The ghosts must be married!—for then there would be no more interference, no more quarreling, no more manifestations and materializations, no more dark séances, with their raps and bells and tambourines and banjos. At first the ghosts would not hear of it. The voice in the corner declared that the Duncan wraith had never thought of matrimony. But Eliphalet argued with them, and pleaded and persuaded and coaxed, and dwelt on the advantages of matrimony. He had to confess, of course, that he did not know how to get a clergyman to marry them; but the voice from the corner gravely told him that there need be no difficulty in regard to that, as there was no lack of spiritual chaplains. Then, for the first time, the house ghost spoke, in a low, clear, gentle voice, and with a quaint, old-fashioned New England accent, which contrasted sharply with the broad Scotch speech of the family ghost. She said that Eliphalet Duncan seemed to have forgotten that she was married. But this did not upset Eliphalet at all; he remembered the whole case clearly, and he told her she was not a married ghost, but a widow, since her husband had been hung for murdering her. Then the Duncan ghost drew attention to the great disparity of their ages, saying that he was nearly four hundred and fifty years old, while she was barely two hundred. But Eliphalet had not talked to juries for nothing; he just buckled to, and coaxed those ghosts into matrimony. Afterward he came to the conclusion that they were willing to be coaxed, but at the time he thought he had pretty hard work to convince them of the advantages of the plan."

"Did he succeed?" asked Baby Van Rensselaer, with a young lady's interest in matrimony.

"He did," said Uncle Larry. "He talked the wraith of the Duncans and the specter of the little old house at Salem into a matrimonial engagement. And from the time they were engaged he had no more trouble with them. They were rival ghosts no longer. They were married by their spiritual chaplain the very same day that Eliphalet Duncan met Kitty Sutton in front of the railing of Grace Church. The ghostly bride and bridegroom went away at once on their bridal tour, and Lord and Lady Duncan went down to the little old house at Salem to pass their honeymoon."

Uncle Larry stopped. His tiny cigar was out again. The tale of the rival ghosts was told. A solemn silence fell on the little party on the deck of the ocean steamer, broken harshly by the hoarse roar of the fog-horn.

# THE NIGHT AT THE HOGG

by Bill Wright

W E HAD BEEN DRIVING ABOUT THREE HOURS, following Highway 108 through the swamps west of New Orleans, when we finally found the country road that leads to the plantation colloquially known as The Hogg.

The ancient road was badly eroded, and after several miles, we were finally forced to park the car beneath a moss-covered oak and walk the rest of the way.

That region must be one of the loneliest in the country. As my wife and I walked, we saw no one, the houses that line that dismal road being vacant—and badly decayed. A few were no more than weed-covered foundations.

When, around four, the great house itself appeared, its hip roof rising above the surrounding forests, I felt, despite my brave talk, a growing sense of apprehension.

"It's an ugly-looking place, isn't it?" my wife asked. "I'd hate to see it at night."

I had come to The Hogg to finish a project I had started more than seven years before, my goal being to photograph every remaining plantation in the Southern United States. I had started in Georgia, and by the time my wife and I reached The

Hogg on December 3, 1982, I had photographed plantations in fourteen states, including Oklahoma and West Virginia.

And yet, I had never seen a place like The Hogg. Over the years, the massive house had sunk into the marsh. Indeed, the ground floor was lost to view. The Corinthian columns that lined the front of the house, however, were still standing though they were leaning at a seemingly impossible angle. Mother Nature, eager to reclaim her own, had covered the sinking house in poisonous-looking vines, which were gradually pulling the house apart. It was as if some vengeful thing buried in the Earth were dragging the house into its grave.

"I don't like this place," my wife said, peering through one of the broken windows. "I feel like someone's watching us."

I rolled my eyes. Linda had not wanted to come on this trip. She was bored of the project, and I was growing tired of her constant complaining and her superstitious rambling.

"It's a miserable place," I said, walking around the side of the house. "You're right about that."

"But you don't feel ... a presence?"

I snorted.

"Of course not. No one lives within twenty miles of this place."

Linda sat down on the trunk of a fallen tree and, taking a pack of cigarettes out of her purse, began to smoke. She seemed genuinely nervous.

"I'm not saying there's an *actual* presence here," she said irritably. "I said that I feel as if we're being watched. It's a feeling, Karl, a sensation. Think of the people who lived here— unwillingly. You don't feel—I don't know—a sense of unease?"

Truthfully, the house did, more so than most of the ruined plantations I had seen, exude a sort of ... unpleasantness, but I didn't want to encourage my wife's neurotic fantasies.

"It's a house, darling, a pile of wood and nails. The people who lived here died a long time ago. Death liberated them. It set them free."

"Yet I can see the old master," my wife murmured, staring at the old house, "in my mind's eye. I can see him standing in front of the window, his whip dangling from his belt."

I scoffed but didn't say anything. I knew better than to encourage her.

I took a few photos of the east wing while my wife, watching me from where she sat, smoked sullenly. In the back, there were more than a dozen dilapidated cabins, a barn, a smokehouse, and a few other ruined buildings. For whatever reason, the whole complex smelled rather foul. I wondered if an animal had died after becoming trapped in one of the buildings.

There was only a little daylight left, and though I would've liked to have photographed the interior of that magnificent and evil-looking edifice, I knew my wife was eager to leave the place. As the sun sank beneath the marsh, I packed up my cameras, tripod, and lens. A few minutes later, we were walking towards the car that would take us back to civilization.

Suddenly, my wife stopped. She was standing in the middle of the road, staring at one of the oak trees that grew along the fence.

"It's not here," she said.

"What are you talking about?"

"The car. It's not here."

"That's not where we parked it, Linda. That's a different tree."

She seemed suddenly irritated.

"Don't be stupid, Karl. You can see our tire marks in the grass."

Shaking slightly, I bent down. There, in the weeds, was the cigarette my wife had smoked before we left the car. I could still the smudge left by her lipstick.

"Someone stole it," I said helplessly. "Someone must live in one of those houses we saw. They followed us. They watched us leave the car. Then they took it."

"Don't be stupid, Karl. No one is living in any of those houses. My God, we didn't pass a single house that still had a roof."

I stood up. My legs were still shaking.

"What do you want me to say, Linda? If someone didn't steal the car, what happened to it? Hmm? What other explanation is there?"

Linda looked at me.

"The place is haunted," I said bitterly. "Is that what you want me to say? That's ridiculous, Linda."

She sat down in the middle of the road. She tried to light another cigarette, but her hands were shaking too much. She could barely hold onto her lighter. Finally, overcome with frustration, she tossed the cigarette away and buried her head in her hands.

"Good God, Karl, what have you gotten us into? Why did you bring me here?"

I was trying to stay calm. For some reason, I felt strangely upset. The theft of our car had certainly inconvenienced us, but I didn't really feel irritated by the loss. I felt anxious, frightened even, as if we were both in some sort of inescapable danger.

"How far do you think it is to the highway?" I asked, trying to peer down the dusky road. "It can't be more than five or six miles."

"It can't be less than ten," my wife said, her voice sounding very small in the vast darkness that was quickly consuming us. "I looked at the odometer."

"We'll get there," I said firmly. "That's all that matters. When we do, we'll find someone who'll drive us into town."

Linda looked up, but she didn't move.

"Come on," I said, giving her my hand. "You don't want me to leave you here, do you?"

She stood up; I shouldered my camera bag; and the two of us began walking down the road.

Around ten o'clock, we turned back.

Linda was shaking so badly she could hardly walk.

"It's not here," she kept murmuring to herself. "It's gone—like the car. It's just gone."

I tried to calm her down, but I, too, was growing frightened. It just didn't make sense.

"The highway's farther away than we thought it was. That's all. There's nothing … weird about that. We miscalculated the distance. Linda, for Christ's sake, be reasonable."

"I saw the odometer, Karl. I know how far it is. We've should've reached the highway two hours ago. It's not here! Why can't you understand that?"

"We've … been walking slowly," I said hesitantly. "That's all. That's all there is to it, Linda."

She laughed. Her voice sounded eerie in that dark and lonesome place.

"It's gone, Paul! There's no point looking for it. It's not where it was or where it should be. We might as well give in—and go back."

My mouth felt dry. I was glad Linda couldn't see my face in the darkness.

"It's not a bad idea," I said, trying to keep my voice steady. "It's really not. We'll sleep in a shed or something—anything with a roof. In the morning, we'll be refreshed. You can wait at the house while I try to find the highway."

Linda said nothing. For a moment, I wasn't sure she was still there.

"It's the only option, isn't it?" I said miserably. "We can't spend the night in the road—there are snakes—and we can't keep walking."

"It's the only option," she repeated listlessly. "It's what he wants."

My watch must have been broken for it took us less than an hour to walk back to the plantation. I wanted Linda to wait for me in the yard in front of the house, which was less overgrown than the rest of the property, but she refused. I took her by the hand, and the two of us, proceeding slowly through the brush with the help of a miniature flashlight, began to explore the outbuildings behind the house.

Most of the barns and sheds had, like the house itself, sunk into the marshy soil. The fields themselves were now shallow ponds. When I first saw them glimmering in the moonlight, my overactive imagination thought the blackish lumps that dotted the fields were the floating corpses of slaves. Then I saw one of the things open its eyes, and I realized that the ponds were filled with alligators.

"Some of the cabins," I began, staring apprehensively at my wife, "seem sound. I think they'll be okay for tonight."

Linda didn't say anything. On the way back to the plantation, she had hardly spoken.

Leaving my wife on the steps, I explored the largest of the cabins with my flashlight. It seemed dry enough inside, and though I wouldn't have been surprised if rattlesnakes were living in the crawlspace beneath the building, I didn't see any wildlife or any traces of wildlife in the cabin itself.

The bed had been removed, but there were still a few pieces of furniture left inside the cabin, including a trunk, a round, three-legged table, and a pair of chairs. After my wife was settled in the corner, I dragged the heavy trunk over to the door, so no one could open the it from the outside. Why I did this, I don't know. No one lived within miles of that place, and even if someone had, they would never have visited it at night.

I broke up one of the flimsy chairs and piled the wood in the fireplace, but when my wife saw what I was doing, she became almost frantic.

"We need a good fire," I said, shaking her off. "It's gloomy in here. A warm fire will cheer the place up a bit."

Even in the inky blackness of that hovel, I could see Linda's eyes grow wide.

"Don't do it, Karl—for the love of God! He'll see!"

"Stop it, Linda! Have you lost your mind? Sit down and let me work."

I fetched an old paperback novel from my camera bag, tore out several pages from the introduction, and lit them with a match. The wood from the chair smoldered for a minute or two, but it finally caught, and soon we had a pleasant fire crackling in the grate.

The inside of the cabin, however, once properly lit, was ghastly. There was nothing—overtly—disquieting about the place. Aside from the furniture mentioned, the interior was bare. And yet ... there *was* something wrong. As old as that miserable place was, it should've seemed as if it were from another age. It should've been—or seemed like—an anachronism, a fragment from a distant and an unreachable past. But it didn't seem like that at all. There were no signs of the present in that place—no graffiti, no broken glass, no trash or needles or bottles or cans. My wife and I were the only anachronisms. We had intruded into a past that, somehow, seemed more like the present, as if that long country road had led, not through space, but through time.

To make matters worse, it didn't take long for the sounds to begin.

I heard it first—a sad song sung by someone way out in the marshy fields. I tried to distract Linda. I talked, as loudly and as confidently as I could, about whatever came to mind, spouting nonsense about current events and family members and old friends. But it was no good. When she heard it, her whole body stiffened. Her face grew pale, as if bleach were pouring through her veins.

Every now and then, a whip split the air.

"They're outside," Linda murmured, her eyes staring at the shuttered window, "in the fields."

"There's no one there," I said, speaking to myself as much as to Linda. "There's nothing."

In time, the singing grew faint, as if the singers had moved farther away. Then it stopped. I made Linda lie down, and she soon fell into an uneasy sleep.

I moved the table, flimsy though it was, in front of the door, and then I snapped another of the chairs into pieces and threw the spindles into the fire. I tried reading the novel I had brought, but I couldn't. I looked at my watch: none of its hands seemed to be moving.

Then Linda began to talk in her sleep—something she never did. At first, I could only make out a few words, but after a while, I thought I could understand her. She was begging, pleading with someone not to do something. Her whimpering became frightful, and I longed for her to be quiet. Finally, overcome with anxiety and fear, I rose from my spot in front of the fire and, bending down, slapped the yellow-pine floorboard next to her ear. Her reaction was astonishing.

She screamed, as if she had been shot or stabbed, the expression on her face indescribable. Her eyes popped open, and her fingers grabbed me by the ankle. I tried to comfort her, but she began to shake all over, as if she were suddenly and horribly cold. Then her back arched; her pupils rolled back into her head; and she groaned. When I touched her arm, she was as stiff as a corpse.

Disturbed by what I had seen, I sat down by the fire. Why had I come to this awful place, I wondered. Why had I chosen to dabble in places so old and ugly? And then, at that moment, something occurred to me. I dragged my camera bag in front of the fire and pulled out my notes. There was something about The Hogg—something unusual—something awful and deadly.

It was there. It was right there in my notes. When, nearly a month after the armistice, the master of the plantation learned that the war was over, he and his brothers dragged the slaves out of their cabins—the men, the women, and the children—and they shot them, one at a time, in the back of the head.

I carefully replaced my notes, my hands trembling slightly, and pushed the camera bag away.

Hours passed though I have no idea how many. At times, I heard voices, as if men and women were talking just outside the cabin's thin walls. I must have fallen asleep, for shortly after sunrise, I woke up—very suddenly and very completely. The fire had died, but in the dim light seeping through the cracks in the walls, I could see Linda sitting up in the corner, her face a sagging mask.

From outside came the sound of hooves. A horseman, riding hard, rode into the farmyard. There was silence and then a low murmur. I could hear the rattle of spurs and the heavy tread of a booted man. A loud knock shook the air, and then I heard the door of one of the cabins creak open. A woman began to scream.

Another door opened. People were yelling. A whip cracked—once—twice—three times.

There was a moment of silence. Then I heard spurs clink against the wooden steps outside our cabin. Something solid, like the butt of a whip, pounded against the door.

"He's here," Linda murmured, "the master."

I felt feverish. The room was growing hot.

"There's no one there!" I shouted at the door.

The pounding continued. It had grown louder. The door was rattling pitifully.

Then I heard the voice. It was like the croaking of some long-dead thing.

Suddenly, the door split. Then it burst open. A dark thing, broad in the shoulder but stooped and somehow crooked, stepped across the threshold. Strong hands grabbed me; a whip cracked, its leather lashing me across the face; and my head rolled backwards. I saw nothing else.

Consciousness, if consciousness it was, returned slowly, painfully. Someone nearby dragged me to my feet, and I found myself standing in a muddy field. Linda, her eyes protruding hideously from her putty-like face, was lying face up in the mud.

She was not the only one. To my left, there was a row of bodies lying on the ground. Some of them were staring at the sky, others at the distant trees that marked the edge of the plantation. Some, couples evidently, were holding hands, their eyes closed, their lips parted slightly, as if they were in mid prayer.

And then, I was running. I was running, my shoes slipping in the mud and the blood and the gore, my heart pounding in my chest. Somewhere nearby, a rifle thundered. I stumbled, slipped, and then I was running again. Gunpowder filled my nostrils. Everywhere, dogs were barking. Men were shouting to one another. Screaming. Crying. Everything seemed dark. Then I saw the fence—the trees. They rose up, and then I was through the fence and among the oaks. The rifle thundered again. A sapling to my right exploded. The darkness at the edge of my vision bled into the center, and I, tumbling, plunged into the forest.

They say a fisherman found me in the marsh, but I don't remember that, nor do I remember much about the two weeks I spent recovering in the hospital. The police say I drove Linda to The Hogg on December 3 and, after raping her, shot her in the back of the head. Perhaps I did. The car, after all, was found less than a mile from the plantation, parked beneath a moss-covered oak tree. I know only that, during the trial, I read as much about The Hogg as I could, and I learned that, despite what I had previously been told, there had been one survivor: a thirty-year-old slave named Oliver Bell, a man whose features, despite being of a different race, are not so unlike my own.

# MRS. DAVENPORT'S GHOST

by Frederick P. Schrader

D EAR READERS, DO YOU AGREE WITH HAMLET? DO you believe that there is more between heaven and earth than we dream of in our philosophy? Does it seem possible to you that Eliphas Levy conjured up the shade of Apollonius of Tyana, the prophet of the Magii, in a London hotel, and that the great sage, William Crookes, drank his tea at breakfast several days a week, for months in succession, in the society of the materialized spirit of a young lady, attired in white linen, with a feather turban on her head?

Do not laugh! Panic would seize you in the presence even of a turbaned spirit, and the grotesque spectacle would but intensify your terror. As for me, I did not laugh last night on reading an account in a New York newspaper of a criminal trial that will probably terminate in the death penalty of the accused.

It is a sad case. I shudder as I transcribe the records of the trial from the testimony of the hotel waiter, who heard the conversation of the two confederates through a keyhole, and of forty thoroughly credible witnesses, who testified to the same facts. What would be my feelings if I had seen the beautiful victim with the gaping wound in her breast, into which she dipped her finger to mark the brow of her murderer?

* * *

About three o'clock on the afternoon of February 3, Professor Davenport and Miss Ida Soutchotte, a very pale and delicate young girl, who had submitted to the tests of Professor Davenport for a number of years, were finishing their dinner in their room in the second story of a New York hotel. Professor Benjamin Davenport was a celebrity, but it was said that he owed his fame to somewhat questionable means. The leading spiritualists did not repose the confidence in him that manifestly marked their regard for William Crookes or Daniel Douglas Home.

"Greedy and unscrupulous mediums," the author of Spiritualism in America thinks, "are to blame for the most bitter attacks to which our cause has been exposed. When the materializations do not take place as quickly as circumstances require, they resort to trickery and fraud to extricate themselves from a dilemma."

Professor Benjamin Davenport belonged to these "versatile" mediums. Aside from this, queer stories were afloat about him. He was secretly accused of highway robbery in South America, cheating at cards in the gambling houses of San Francisco, and the overhasty use of firearms toward persons who had never offended him. It was said almost openly, that the professor's wife had died from abuse and grief at his infidelity. But in spite of these annoying rumors, Mr. Davenport, by virtue of his skill as a fraud and fakir, continued to exercise a great deal of influence upon certain plain and simple-minded folks, whom it was impossible to convince that they had not touched the materialized spirits of their brothers, mothers, or sisters through the agency of his wonderful power. His professional success

50

received material accession from his swarthy, Mephisto-like countenance, his deep, fiery eyes, his large curved nose, the cynical expression of his mouth, and the lofty, almost prophetic tone of his words.

When the waiter had made his last visit—he did not go far—the following conversation took place in the room:

"There is to be a seance this evening at the residence of Mrs. Harding," began the medium. "Quite a number of influential people will be there, and two or three millionaires. Conceal under your skirt the blonde woman's wig and the white material in which the spirits usually make their appearance."

"Very well," replied Ida Soutchotte, in a resigned tone.

The waiter heard her pace the room. After a pause, she asked:

"Whose spirit are you going to control this evening, Benjamin?"

The waiter heard a loud, brutal laugh and the chair groaning beneath the weight of the demonstrative professor.

"Guess."

"How should I know?" she asked.

"I am going to conjure up the spirit of my dead wife."

And another burst of laughter issued from the room, full of sinister levity. A cry of terror burst from Ida's lips. A muffled sound indicated to the eavesdropper at the door that she was dragging herself to the feet of the professor.

"Benjamin, Benjamin! don't do it," she sobbed.

"Why not? They say I broke Mrs. Davenport's heart. The story is damaging my reputation, but it will be forgotten if her spirit should address me in terms of endearment from the other shore in the presence of numerous witnesses. For you will speak to me tenderly, will you not, Ida?"

"No, no. You shall not do it; you shall not think of it. Listen to me, for God's sake. During the four years that I have been with you I have obeyed you faithfully and suffered patiently. I have lied and deceived, like you; I learned to imitate the sleep and symptoms of clairvoyants. Tell me, did I ever refuse to serve you, or utter a word of complaint, even when my shoulders bent with the weight of my burden, when you pierced the flesh of my arms with knitting needles? Worse than all this, I imitated distant voices behind curtains, and made mothers and wives believe that their sons and husbands had come from a better world to communicate with them. How often have I performed the most dangerous feats in parlors with the lamps turned low? Clothed in a shroud or white muslin I essayed to represent supernatural forms, whom tear-dimmed eyes recognized as those of departed dear ones. You do not know what I suffered at this unhallowed work. You scoff at the mysteries of eternity. I suffer the torments of an impending retribution. My God! if some time the dead whom I counterfeit should rise up before me with uplifted arms and dreadful imprecations! This constant terror has injured my heart—it will kill me. I am consumed by fever. Look how emaciated, how worn-out and downcast I am. But I am under your control. Do as you like with me; I am in your power, and I want it to be so. Have I ever complained? But do not force me to do this thing, Benjamin. Have pity on me for what I have done for you in the past, for what I am suffering. Do not attempt this mummery; do not compel me to play the role of your dead wife, who was so tender and beautiful. Oh, what put that thought into your mind? Spare me, Benjamin, I implore you!"

The professor did not laugh again. Amid the confusion of upturned articles of furniture the eavesdropper distinguished the sound of a skull striking the floor. He concluded that Professor Davenport had knocked Miss Ida down with a blow of his fist, or had kicked her as she approached him. But the waiter did not enter the room, as no one rang for him.

* * *

That evening forty persons were assembled in Mrs. Joanne Harding's parlor, staring at the curtain where a spirit form was in process of materializing. One dark lantern in a corner of the room contributed the light that emphasized the darkness rather than relieved it. The room was pervaded by profound silence, save the quickened, suppressed breathing of the spectators. The fire in the grate cast mysterious rays of light, resembling fugitive spirits, upon the objects around, almost indistinguishable in the semi-gloom.

Professor Davenport was at his best this evening. The spirit world obeyed him without hesitation, like their lawful master. He was the mighty prince of souls. Hands that had no arms were seen picking flowers from the vases; the touch of an invisible spirit conjured sweet melodies from the keys of the piano; the furniture responded by intelligent rappings to the most unanticipated questions. The professor himself elevated his form in symbolical distortions from the floor to an altitude of three feet, indicated by Mrs. Harding, and remained suspended in the air for a quarter of an hour, holding live coals in his hands.

* * *

But the most interesting, as well as the most conclusive, test was to be the materialization of the spirit of Mrs. Arabella Davenport, which the professor had promised at the beginning of the seance.

"The hour has come," exclaimed the medium.

And while the hearts of all throbbed with anxious suspense, and their eyes distended with painful expectancy of the promised materialization, Benjamin Davenport stood before the curtain. In the twilight the tall man with the disheveled hair and demon look, was really terrible and handsome.

"Appear, Arabella!" he exclaimed, in a commanding voice, with gestures of the Nazarene at the sepulcher of Lazarus.

All are waiting——

Suddenly a cry burst from behind the curtain—a piercing, shuddering, horrible shriek, the shriek of an expiring soul.

The spectators trembled. Mrs. Harding almost fainted. The medium himself appeared surprised.

But Benjamin recovered his composure on seeing the curtain move and admit the spirit.

The apparition was that of a young woman with long blonde tresses; she was beautiful and pale, clad in some light, whitish material. Her breast was bare, and on the left side appeared a bleeding wound, in which trembled a knife.

The spectators arose and retreated, pushing their chairs to the wall. Those who chanced to look at the medium noticed that a deathly pallor had overspread his face, and that he was cowering and trembling.

But the young woman, Mrs. Arabella, the real one, whom he so well remembered, she had come in response to his summons, and advanced in a direct line toward Benjamin, who in terror covered his eyes to shut out the ghastly sight, and with a cry fled behind the furniture. But she dipped the finger of her thin hand into the blood from her wound and traced it across the brow of the unconscious medium, the while repeating, in a slow, monotonous tone that sounded like the echo of a wail, again and again:

"You are my murderer! You are my murderer!"

And while he was rolling and tossing in deadly terror on the floor they turned up the lights.

The spirit had vanished. But in the communicating room, behind the curtain, they found the body of poor Miss Ida Soutchotte with horribly distorted features. A physician who was present pronounced it heart stroke.

And that is the reason that Prof. Benjamin Davenport appeared alone in a New York courtroom to answer to the charge of having murdered his wife four years ago in San Francisco.

# THE GIVERS

by John S. Price

JIM WALLACE LOOKED WORRIED. EVERY NOW AND then, he would run his long fingers through his hair and lick his lips, as if he were agitated or dumbfounded. Then he would mutter into his beard or scratch his head or twist the end of his tie. Wallace was a scrawny man, shorter than most women, but wiry and strong. He was rarely rattled.

"I think we should kill it," he said finally.

Paul Iverson and I looked at him.

"What are you talking about?" Iverson asked. "What do you mean we should kill it?"

The three of us were sitting in Paul's office on the third floor of Crimson Hall, the oldest building on campus and home to the university's department of psychology.

"We'll tell the government it was an accident," Wallace said, fingering the end of his tie. "No one—outside of this room— needs to know that we did it deliberately."

Iverson bit his lip. He looked furious.

"Why?" he asked simply.

Wallace stood up and, wiping the sweat from his brow, began to pace up and down the room.

"I don't like it," he said, speaking—as far as I could tell—to himself. "I don't like the thing. It's an ugly thing—you can't deny that. And I don't like the way it listens. I talked to it for almost four hours yesterday. I don't know that anyone in this country has talked to one of those things for as long as I have. I told it more than I should have maybe, but I don't think.... I don't think we're lost—not yet. But we should kill it. You and I should do it, Paul. We can't.... We can't.... We can't keep something like that here."

Iverson and I glanced at one another. Wallace's reaction, as insane as it sounded, was not entirely a surprise. Iverson had theorized, not long after the first of the things was found, that prolonged interaction with an alien consciousness would be disorienting—and possibly dangerous.

"Jim, please. Sit down. Calm down. We need to discuss this rationally. That's better. Now tell me exactly what, uh, the two of you discussed."

Wallace had returned to his seat, but he couldn't sit still. His antique chair creaked every time he moved.

"I tried to talk to it about politics—guardedly, of course—but it wasn't interested. I tried to talk about history, but—I swear to God, Paul—the thing seemed bored. I couldn't get it to talk. It just squatted in the corner—like some sort of poisonous toad."

Iverson leaned back in his chair. His gray hair was almost white in the afternoon sunlight pouring through the window behind his desk.

"That's no surprise. We've known for some time that these ... creatures ... aren't interested in abstractions."

"No," Wallace whispered to himself, "they're not interested in abstractions. They're more interested in ... domestic affairs."

Wallace was looking down at his tie. He seemed suddenly deflated.

Iverson watched him for a long time. Then he cleared his throat and, leaning forward, put his hands on his desk.

"I don't want you talking to it alone," he said firmly. "From now on, Kirby will accompany you. He'll be there for every session."

"I don't need him," Wallace snapped. "I can handle the thing by myself."

Iverson's right eyebrow rose. A look of mirth passed across his otherwise serious face.

"We don't know if anyone can handle these things, Jim. It may be that mankind isn't meant to interact with … things from outside. Man was, until about eighteen months ago, an orphan in this universe. Now, for the first time in history, we're talking to an animal that actually listens—and talks back. Are these interactions good for us? Are they good for them? These are the questions we have to answer."

"I still don't understand," I said, shifting uncomfortably in my chair. "Why wouldn't these interactions be positive? People talk to their dogs all the time. How is this any different?"

Iverson and Wallace exchanged glances.

"Do you remember," Paul began quietly, his eyes looking away from mine, "when one of the astronauts aboard the Argosy died shortly before reentry?"

"Of course."

"His appendix didn't burst. He committed suicide, Kirby. He killed himself."

I was stunned. The entire nation had mourned the sudden death of Colonel George Finley, the first man to ever encounter an alien lifeform.

I started to say something, but Iverson, with a wave of his hand, cut me off.

"This doesn't leave this room, Kirby. I don't ever want to hear you talk about this with anyone else. I know. Wallace knows. He needed to know. If you're going to assist him, you need to know. No one else does. Do you understand?"

"I don't think I do—not really. Finley's death was tragic, of course, but—"

"The thing is…. Finley left a suicide note. I've read it—so has Jim. It's mostly gibberish—weird stuff—but he places all the blame on … one of those things."

I was speechless. I didn't know how to respond.

"That's why we have one here—at the college. We need to understand how they interact with humans and how we interact with them."

I nodded and, rising to leave, looked over at Wallace. He was staring at the distant hills through the window, a faraway look in his milky blue eyes.

* * *

"Are you sure you want to go in?" Wallace asked, pausing in front of the door. "You could tell Iverson that you did. I would cover for you."

I had always liked Wallace, but he was beginning to irritate me. Though undoubtedly brilliant, he didn't deserve sole access to something like this—something that should have been shared with the entire department.

"I'll be fine," I said. "Trust me. I've been looking forward to this."

Wallace looked at me as if I had said something unbelievably bizarre. Then he turned the key and, with a soft sigh, pushed open the heavy door.

The room was dark, a single bulb, partially obscured by artificial rocks, being the only light source. Enormous shadows, which I assumed were boulders, occupied most of the room, leaving only a narrow track for us to traverse. Somewhat nervous, I hurried after Wallace, who had almost disappeared down the trail. When I finally caught up with him, he was sitting on the sandy floor, his back propped up by a broken column.

I looked around, but I couldn't see anything in the dark. If there was an alien entity in this weird room, it wasn't making itself visible.

"You don't really get a sense of what its world is like from the pictures," I murmured. "It's a nasty place, isn't it?"

Wallace ignored me. He was staring, his mouth slightly open, at a lump of glistening rock about three yards in front of him. Only when the thing twitched did I realize it was alive.

Its yellowish eyes flickering, the toad-like thing began to croak.

Wallace flinched. Then, as if obeying orders, he began to talk. I expected him to discuss cultural practices or perhaps even religious beliefs, but he didn't. He started talking about the day, nearly four years ago, he found out that his wife was cheating on him.

When, after about an hour, he had finished, he slouched forward, as if the process had exhausted him.

To my surprise, the thing on the rock turned towards me. I could see it better now. It was larger than the ones I had seen on television, being about the size of a newborn baby. As small as it was, it was so oddly proportioned that it seemed monstrously fat, consisting almost entirely of an immense, bloated body. The head, however, was the worst part, for it seemed to be nothing but an enormous mouth on top of which rested a pair of perfectly round eyes. My impression, influenced no doubt by the alien room in which I found myself, was of a mechanical entity, lacking in intelligence or consciousness and yet possessing a malignant or malevolent will.

"Tell me," the alien croaked.

Terrified, I could hardly move. I knew, of course, that the things had learned to talk—to form crude words in the English language, but to actually hear and understand a creature from another world was overwhelming. I felt faint—and sick.

"Is this what your world is like?" I asked, gesturing at the lichen-covered ruins which surrounded us. "The city where you were found—did your people build it?"

The toad seemed to swell, as if angry. Then it shriveled up, blinked its greasy eyes, and began, very softly, to buzz.

"The astronauts," I said, hypnotized by the weird sound, "aboard the Argosy found the ruins of a temple. Is that what it was? Do your people believe in God? A.... A sort of supreme being ... a master or creator?"

The thing was staring at me. The awful buzzing sound it was making had grown louder. I looked over at Wallace, but he was slouched against the column. His eyes were open, but he seemed only partially conscious.

"Why ... do you make that sound?" I asked, feeling increasingly nauseous. "Could you.... Could you stop doing that?"

The thing stopped for a moment. Then, to my horror, it waddled forward until it was within a yard of my face. Then it opened its enormous mouth....

"Tell me," it croaked.

I started to respond. I started to ask the creature about the history of its race, about its culture, its religion, its sense of morality. Only gradually did I realize that I wasn't talking about any of those things. I was talking about something seemingly insignificant: the time, years ago, when I had witnessed a car accident. A little girl, about four years old, had died in that crash. I had helped pull her mangled body from the car.

"I want," I said, my head spinning, "to ask you … about your planet. I want to know about … how you live."

But the thing had waddled away. It squeezed its fat bulk between two stone blocks and disappeared. After a while, I began to hear a gurgling sound, as if it were digesting a large and savory meal.

*** * ***

I was sitting in Paul Iverson's kitchen while his wife, a woman about my age whom Paul had met at Ann Arbor, prepared dinner. Paul, who was sitting to my left, was shucking corn.

"I don't think Wallace is doing well," I said, looking down at the watch the department had given me. "He seems—oh, I don't know—unhealthy, I guess."

Iverson didn't say anything at first, but I could tell that he wasn't happy.

"I'd say he seems happy, happier than I've seen him in a long time anyway. Wouldn't you say so, honey?"

His wife nodded but didn't stop what she was doing.

"Definitely. He seems younger, too. He was over here last week, you know. I don't think I've ever seen him in such good spirits. He was laughing and joking. I've never seen him like that. He used to be so serious."

"I know," I said, aware of how foolish I sounded. "He does seem—outwardly—more … cheerful. But … I think there's something wrong with him."

Paul looked up from the ear of corn he was shucking.

"A month ago, he told us that he wanted to kill Argus. He wanted us to murder him and lie about it to the government. But you think that, since then, he's changed for the worse."

"I do."

"How?" he asked, exasperated.

"I don't know, but he's not well. These sessions…. They're not good for him."

Iverson slowly put the ear of corn down on the table. Then he pushed his chair back and, folding his arms across his chest, stared at me.

"I've read your notes. I've listened to the recordings. I've examined—don't interrupt—Wallace's test results. He's scoring higher—way higher—than he did when the sessions began. You both are. He's healthy, Kirby. He's getting *better.*"

"Why?" I asked, suddenly excited. "Why does … this *thing* … want to hear about his divorce? About his father's death? About the time he almost choked to death? Why does it want to know about his personal life? I've tried—God knows I've tried—to interest it in politics, science, art…. It never asks about any of those things."

Iverson sighed. He glanced at his wife, as if I were a child to whom the simplest matters had to be explained.

"Higher lifeforms," he began slowly, "aren't interested in mechanics, Kirby. When was the last time you wanted to talk about addition or subtraction or … or … how levers work? Argus, and his people, have evolved beyond that. The minutia of government, of history, of theology—these things would be of no interest to advanced civilizations."

"It's not," I said patiently, "interested in the minutia of history, but it *is* interested in the minutia of daily life?"

Iverson nodded and then, picking up the ear of corn he had laid on the table, resumed his work.

"They've reached a level of civilization above ours. They have, I suspect, highly developed emotional lives—and a strong sense of empathy."

"But why does Argus never ask about anything ... positive?"

Iverson must have heard me, but he didn't answer. And I didn't ask again.

* * *

When I arrived at Crimson Hall, two graduate students were carrying the thing through the hallway on a stretcher. It was about the size of a four-year-old child.

I found Wallace nearby. He was sitting on the floor in front of the door. He had been crying.

"I'm cancelling the one-on-one sessions," Iverson said. "I'm disassembling all of this ... junk. We're not learning anything, Kirby. The specimen at Berkeley has already started living with a human colleague."

"It lives," I asked, mesmerized, "in someone's house?"

Iverson nodded.

"In a guest bedroom. It's responded marvelously well. It sleeps in a bed. It eats ... whatever the family eats. It's like a retriever, Kirby. And we've been keeping it in a goddamn terrarium, as if it were a rattlesnake."

"But we are learning things," I said, suddenly desperate. "We're learning so much. Jim and I—we just need more time with it. That's all."

Iverson gave me a piercing look.

"You and Jim have been starving it. It craves companionship, Kirby, and you've been keeping it locked up in a closet. Something like this needs to be shared with the world—for its benefit as well as ours. I'm going to initiate group sessions."

"I want to take part," I blurted out. "Argus and I have a rapport."

Iverson nodded. Then, with a wave of his hand, he dismissed me. There was a time when his disrespect would have injured me, but I didn't mind it now. It didn't bother me at all.

* * *

"I've seen them," I said, closing the door behind me. "There are fourteen of them out there. I've been coaching them. There's a girl—a beautiful young girl—who was raped when she was just a child. And there's a boy…. Oh, you'll love him. There are cuts up and down his arm. Listen, I know how much you miss Jim, but there are plenty of others—millions. And they'll learn to appreciate you like I do."

The floor creaked as the thing shifted its weight. Its mossy eyes stared into mine.

"We still have a minute or two left, don't we? I know you're hungry. Let me tell you about the most delicious pain."

I knelt down and, resting my forehead against the thing's face, began to stroke its warty head.

# COMPENSATION

### by Charles V. Tench

W HY, JOHN!" INVOLUNTARILY I HALTED AT THE
entrance to my snug bachelor quarters as the flood of
light my turning of the switch produced revealed a huddled
figure slumped in an easy chair.

"Aye, sir, 'tis me." The man got to his feet, gnarled hands
rubbing at his eyes. "An' 'tis all day that I've been waiting for
you, sir. The caretaker said you'd be back soon so let me in. I
must have fell asleep, an' no wonder, what with the strain an' no
sleep or rest all last night."

"Strain? No rest?" I stared my bewilderment, trying at the
same time to conceal the vague apprehensions occasioned by
the fact that the trusted servitor of my friend, Professor
Wroxton, should wait all day for me.

Hastily shedding my outer things, I bade him again be
seated, sat down facing him, and asked him to explain.

"'Tis the professor, sir." The old chap peered at me with
anxious, wrinkled eyes. "'Tis common enough for him to send
me here on messages, sir, but to-day I've come on my own,
because, sir," answering the question in my eyes, "I haven't seen
sight of him since last night."

"Why—" I began.

"That's just it, sir." John took the words out of my mouth. "For twenty years my wife an' me have looked after the professor at The Grange. In all that time he's never been away at night. Whenever he had to come to town he'd tell us. Most times I'd drive him myself in the old car. But that was very seldom, sir, for Professor Wroxton had few interests outside."

* * *

"But, John," I protested "is there no other reason for your agitation? He might have had an urgent call, or gone out for a walk or drive by himself."

"No, sir. If you'll pardon me, sir, you're wrong. The professor was fixed in his habits. He would not go away without tellin' me. Think back, sir, you know the professor as well as me. Better, because you are his friend and I am only a servant. Although, sir," this proudly, "he always treated me as a friend."

"Go on," I urged, seeing he was not finished.

"Well, sir, a few minutes back you asked me if there was no other reason for my being upset like. There is, sir. You know, sir, that for more'n twenty years the professor has led a retired sort of life; the life of a—a—"

"Recluse," I suggested.

"That's it, sir. He only left The Grange when he had to. He was all wrapped up in some weird-like thing he was inventing. In all those years, sir, you were the only visitor who ever went into his laboratory, or stayed at The Grange for a night or more. That is, sir, until three days ago."

"Go on," I again urged, some of his perturbation communicating itself to me.

"The Grange, sir, lying as it does, fifteen miles from town an' back in its own grounds away from the road, isn't noted by many.

When strangers do get into the grounds I usually gets 'em out again in short order. Three days ago, sir, a stranger drove up to the door in a fine car. He told me he was wantin' to purchase a country home. I told him The Grange was not for sale an' turned 'im away. He was turning his car to leave when my master came out. To my surprise, sir, he invited the stranger in. An' I'm sure, sir, because he looked so taken aback like, that the stranger had never seen the professor before."

"And after that?" I asked, now feeling decidedly uneasy.

"The stranger, sir—a Mr. Lathom he called himself—stayed on. He was in the study with the master last night. This morning there was no trace of either of them."

"But—good God, John!" I jerked to my feet, a fresh dread clutching at my heart. "What are you trying to get at? The professor and Mr. Lathom might possibly have driven away somewhere last night."

"Both cars, sir," the servant answered, "are in the garage. I bolt all the doors in the house myself every night. They were still fastened this morning. My wife an' me searched the house from cellar to garret an' hunted all over the grounds. We couldn't find a trace of the master or his guest."

"You mean to suggest then," I shot at him, "that two full grown men have completely vanished? It's absurd, John, absurd!"

* * *

I paced the floor thinking desperately for a few minutes, conscious of the ancient's anxious eyes. I half smiled. The thing was too ridiculous for anything. Old John had grown morbid from living away from the outer world. Also, I had to admit that the atmosphere of The Grange, impregnated as it was with the lethal scientific dabblings of my friend, was exactly suited to the conjuring up of unhealthy forebodings in uneducated minds. I'd drive out to the home of my friend at once. No doubt I'd find him fit and well. He had refused to install a phone, so drive it had to be.

"John." I stopped my pacing and patted him on the shoulder. "I'm coming out to The Grange at once." His face showed his thankfulness. "I am sure," I went on as I struggled into my coat, "that we shall find the professor and his guest awaiting us. Anyway, it's time you got back to your wife and had some food."

"I hope to Heaven, sir, that you're right." With that we left the building and entered my car.

Although I had tried to dispel my fears, although I had tried to banter John out of his dread, I drove that evening as I had never driven before or since. Barely fifteen minutes later I halted my roadster at the short flight of steps leading to the main door of The Grange. Even as we stepped from the machine the door flung open and an agitated woman hurried towards us. She was Mary, John's wife.

"Sir!" She gripped my arm and stared anxiously into my face. "'Tis glad I am that you've come. The Grange is a house of death."

In spite of myself a chill shook my whole body. Gently handing her to John, I strode up the steps.

At the open doorway I halted, the aged couple crowding on my heels, the woman still babbling about death. I couldn't blame her. All day she had been alone in that gloomy, rambling old building, wondering, no doubt, why John and I had not returned sooner.

* * *

And gloomy the house was. Always, even when staying there at the professor's request, I had found it to be somber and depressing, as if there lurked within its walls the shadowy wings of the years-old tragedy that had caused my friend to retire to such a God-forsaken place, and there become absorbed in his scientific experiments.

Even now, as I gazed into the dimly-lighted hallway, the air seemed charged with that same malignant something I cannot describe.

Pulling myself together I strode quickly along the corridor, and flung open the study door. The lights being full on, one glance sufficed to show me that my friend was not there. Swinging on my heel, the horror I saw in the eyes of the servants, honest, healthy folks not easily frightened, conveyed itself to me. Somehow, the sight of that room, lights on, chairs drawn up to the burnt-out fire, brought home to me the fact that something serious was amiss. I chided myself for thinking John had been unduly agitated.

For a moment I stood, trying to conceal the chill coursing through my veins, puzzling what to do next. I decided to search the house thoroughly. If I found no sign of the professor or his guest, I would call in the police.

Fearfully yet willingly the aged couple led me from room to room, from attic to basement, until but one place remained— the laboratory. I hesitated for several seconds at the closed door of my friend's workroom. Not that I had never entered the—to a layman's eyes—weirdly-appointed place. I had been in many times with the professor. But this time I dreaded what I might find.

* * *

Pulling myself together, I gently tried the door. To my horror it yielded to my touch. Alive, the professor always kept it locked. A new dread assailed me, as, flinging the door wide open, I blinked in the sudden glare of powerful globes. Someone had left the lights full on!

Horrified I stood and stared, knowing by their heavy breathing that the aged couple were also staring with fright-widened eyes. Afraid of what? I did not know. I only knew that the atmosphere had become even more sinister. I knew that something dreadful had taken place in that room.

Trembling with consternation I forced myself to take a few steps forward, then I again stared about me. At one end of the large room something shone brightly in the glow of the lights. Slowly I walked across to examine it: it appeared to be a glass case, almost like a show-case, about eight feet square and seven feet in height. With the mechanical actions of the mentally distraught I walked all around it. Not the slightest sign of an entrance could I see. The fact intrigued me. I tapped lightly on the highly polished surface with my fingers. It rang to my touch like cut glass.

Through the transparent surface I could see John and his wife. They were watching me furtively, wondering, no doubt, why I lingered. As I looked at them John suddenly lumbered up to the case on the opposite side. Dropping to his knees, he stared. Turning an imploring gaze to me, he pointed. His lips moved soundlessly. I followed the pointing finger with my eyes; gasped at what I saw.

Near the center of the cage, on the floor constructed of the same crystalline substance, something glittered, its brilliance almost dazzling as the light rays struck it. My face pressed close to the cold outer surface of the structure, my shocked intelligence gradually realized what that small sparkling object was. It was a magnificent diamond—and the professor had always worn a diamond ring!

* * *

In a sudden frenzy of horror I pawed my way around the cage to where John still knelt. As I reached him he jerked his head in a numb way as he croaked, "It's a diamond, sir! The professor's!"

"But how?" I implored. "How can it be? There's no way into this thing. Perhaps he was working here, and the stone came loose from its setting. He couldn't have dropped it after the cage was completed."

"It's his diamond, sir," intoned the old man, dully. "I know it is."

Then a sudden unreasoning terror filled me. I shrank away from that shining box. It seemed to be mocking me, gloatingly, malevolently.

"Quickly!" I threw at the aged couple. "Let us get out of here! Now! At once!" They needed no second urging. I knew that they felt as I felt: the laboratory was a sepulcher!

Five minutes later I was guiding my car over the narrow road to town. I did not pause until I drew up at police headquarters. I suppose my appearance was distraught, for I was ushered into the presence of the chief without delay. In a few moments I had poured out my story. He listened with a polite calmness I found almost maddening. Leaning back in his chair, he reviewed, audibly, the facts.

"Some twenty-odd years ago your friend, Professor Wroxton, married. He was so absorbed in the pursuit of some weird invention that he neglected his bride. She ran away with another man. This man deserted her, and disappeared. The professor found her many months later, in desperate health. Shortly afterwards she died. Your friend tried to trail the man, but failed. Shocked and saddened beyond measure, he retired to a place known as The Grange."

* * *

He suddenly straightened up in his seat, and pointed at me a thick forefinger.

"How long have you known Professor Wroxton?"

"About ten years," I answered.

"What was he trying to invent?"

"I don't know," I replied.

"And yet you had his confidence in other matters?"

"But what has all this to do with finding out what has become of my friend?" I blurted out. "Perhaps every moment counts."

"A lot." The chief eyed me in a way I did not like. "Solely because your friend has not been seen by his servants for nearly twenty-four hours, merely because you saw what you believe to be his diamond in some kind of a glass compartment in his laboratory, you come here as distraught as a man who has something terrible on his mind. Why?"

"I can't say." I shifted uneasily under that direct stare. "Somehow I *feel* that something dreadful has happened to my friend."

"We do not go by *feelings*." The chief got to his feet. "But you have told me enough to warrant action. I want you to guide me and a couple of men to this house. Please wait here until I return." He left the room.

Sitting there awaiting his return, I tried to ponder the matter reasonably. After all, perhaps the chief was right. Merely because the professor had been absent for a few hours and I had seen what I thought to be his diamond in the laboratory, I had worked myself into a perfect fever of anxiety. I almost smiled to myself. In that businesslike office the whole affair did seem absurd. After all the professor did not have to answer to his servants for his actions.

Heavy footsteps, announcing the chief's return, caused me to rise to my feet. A few minutes later, in company with the three officers, I was driving again towards The Grange.

* * *

We made the return journey in almost complete silence. Occasionally the chief would shoot a question at me; but, the night air cooling my fevered brain, my replies were guarded. He realized that fact, for I felt his eyes upon me all the way. What was going on behind that broad forehead, I wondered.

Then we reached The Grange. As we mounted the steps, John, his wife herding behind him, flung wide the door. He answered the question in my eyes with a negative shake of his head, and the words, "Nothing fresh, sir."

The chief eyed him keenly, then curtly bade him lead the way to the laboratory. John hung back, his face blanched. "I can't, sir," he faltered. The chief turned to me, and, although I wanted to follow John's example, although the atmosphere of the house had again filled me with an unshakable dread, I led the way, standing back at the door to allow the officers to enter first.

With calculating gaze the chief slowly took in every detail of the stone apartment. He turned to me.

"What is there here to be afraid of?" I pointed hesitatingly towards the crystalline cage. The chief and his men strode across to it.

"You don't know how to open this?" the chief shot at me after a brief examination.

"No," I replied. "It was not here on my last visit."

"When was that?"

"Some two or three months ago", I answered. "My work occasions much traveling on my part."

* * *

The chief and his men turned again to the cage, talking in undertones. He turned again to me.

"You notice that this thing is built in sections. One of them must be movable. Perhaps—" He paused as his eyes fell upon some wires and tubes that trailed across the floor from underneath the cage to a switchboard fastened to the wall.

"Perhaps," he repeated, "it is worked from that board." He crossed over, stared thoughtfully at the shining levers for some seconds, and moved one slightly. The result was astounding. All four of us stared with unbelieving eyes as slowly, without the faintest sound, a section of one wall slid inwards, as if guided by invisible tracks on floor and ceiling.

"Guess that's enough for now." With the words the chief backed away, almost timidly, I thought, from the switchboard, and walked to the cage. For a moment he hesitated, but he entered, and emerged with the sparkling object in his hand.

"It's the professor's," I choked, crowding close to him.

"How'd you know?" he shot back. "All unset stones look pretty much alike."

"I just know," was all I could falter.

"You 'just know'." The chief sat down on a stool and regarded me searchingly. "Mr. Thornton, when I started out with you, I thought I was on a wild goose chase or the trail of a confession.

You looked exactly like a man who had either committed a serious crime, or was getting over a bad drunk. I feel sure now"—he again regarded the diamond—"that your story was not the product of an alcohol-crazed brain. Come on!" He lurched to his feet and grasped me by the shoulder. "Come through!"

* * *

Without answering, I wrenched myself free. Over my shoulder I saw one of the policemen at the door. In the hand of the other a revolver suddenly appeared. Good God! I glared in bewilderment from one to another. Was I going mad? Surely this was some awful nightmare! What had I said to make them suspect me of having committed a revolting crime?

"Sit down!" The command came from the chief. Mechanically I found a stool, and obeyed him. "Hold your stations, boys, and listen carefully," he ordered his men. Then he turned to me.

"Professor Wroxton was a wealthy man without kith or kin?"

"Yes."

"Do you know the nature of his will?"

"Yes." Chilled to the heart, I felt the circumstantial net tightening.

"What is its nature?"

"This house and an annuity to John and his wife," I explained. "The residue of his wealth to me."

"Humph!" The chief stared at me piercingly. "And how has business been with you lately?"

Damn the man! What right had he to put me through the third degree? I felt my state of dazed horror slowly giving way to anger. I glanced around. The pistol still menaced; the man at the door had not moved. It was useless to try and evade the questions.

"For the past year," I replied, "business has been very poor. In fact, the professor advanced me some money."

"Humph!" Again that irritating, non-committal grunt.

* * *

The chief turned in his seat and stared thoughtfully at the crystalline cage.

"And you don't know what the professor was trying to invent?"

"Only its nature," I began.

"Ah! That's better. Why didn't you tell me that before?" The chief leaned forward.

"Well," I explained, "the whole thing seems so absurd. When the professor told me how his married life had been broken up, he told me that at that time he reached the utmost depths of human suffering. Absolute zero, he called it."

"Ah!"

"The experiments he indulged in," I continued, trying to hide the shiver pimpling my flesh, "were to produce an actual state of absolute zero. It is years since he told me this. I had almost forgotten it."

"And exactly what is an absolute zero?" The chief's eyes never left mine.

"Well," I protested, "please understand that I also am a layman in these matters. According to my friend, an absolute zero has been the dream of scientists for ages. Once upon a time it was attained, but the secret became lost."

"And exactly what is an absolute zero?"

Curse the man! I could have struck him down for the chilling level of his tone. I forced myself to go on, realizing that I was damning myself at every step.

"An absolute zero is a cold so intense it will destroy flesh, bone and tissue. Remove them," my voice rose in spite of myself, "leaving absolutely no trace."

\* \* \*

No trace! Something attracted my eyes. The chief had opened his hand. The diamond there flashed and sparkled as if mocking me. I pulled myself together, and went on.

"It all comes back to me now. One day I came out here and found the professor terribly distraught. He told me that, with the aid of electric currents he had been able to invent the absolute zero, but he could not invent a *container*."

"Why?" Those eyes continued to bore into mine.

"Because—remember it is years since he told me this—there was difficulty in controlling the power. Besides destroying living things, it would destroy bricks and mortar, stone and iron. Only one substance it could not wipe out—crystalline of diamond hardness.

"I know, now!" I jumped to my feet and grabbed the chief's arm. "I know now what he meant. Fool, fool! Why did I not think of it before? This—" I swung towards the cage—"is compensation." Almost panting in my eagerness I went on:

"My friend told me that the law of compensation would atone to him for the tragedy of his youth. Absolute zero in suffering would be atoned for by a real state of absolute zero. Chief!" I whirled on him. "Don't you understand? This is the perfected dream of my friend. It is the absolute zero."

"Humph! Plausible but not convincing." I slumped back at the officer's words. "That does not explain the professor's disappearance. Even if it did, what about Mr. Lathom? And don't forget this contrivance is worked from outside. We found the diamond inside. Of course, he might have placed it there himself to test the machine," he concluded.

"Of course, that's it," I commenced. But I regretted the words when I saw suspicion flicker again in the chief's eyes. Lamely I finished, "And he has probably rushed off, in an ecstasy of triumph, to acquaint professional colleagues."

"Without unlocking any doors or taking a car, eh?"

"Mr. Thornton." The chief stood up and regarded me sternly. "As a sensible man, don't you think yourself that your story is a bit thin? The professor has disappeared. Here is a strange-looking case which you say is an absolute zero container. Whether you know, or are just jumping at conclusions, remains to be proved. But even if it is, do you think that, after perfecting such a tremendous invention, the professor would commit suicide?"

"On the contrary," I gasped, "my friend was a man of gentle, kindly disposition, but strong purpose. I should think his first action on attaining his life's ambition would be to notify me, his closest friend."

"And he didn't." Every word condemned me, and roused me to retaliate.

"Chief, I know enough of the law to know that, before you can try a man for murder, you must prove that murder has been committed." I grinned savagely. "You must have the corpus delicti. Go ahead! Find my friend or his remains, or else withdraw your charges." I grinned again, with shocked mirthlessness.

* * *

Then I buried my head in my hands. I had called in the police to help find the professor, and they had only blundered around and asked a lot of stupid questions. The chief had practically accused me of murder—something I knew he could not prove, yet feared he might. Because I had told the chief of the locked doors and unused cars, he had confined his investigations to the house itself.

He interrupted my thoughts.

"Mr. Thornton, I am going back to town. You will remain here with my men. I advise you to get some sleep, as I shall not be able to carry out certain investigations until the morning. One of my men will spend his time searching the house and patrolling the grounds, the other one will stay here with you."

He turned away, whispered some instructions to his men, and, followed by one of them, silently left the laboratory. I started to protest, tried to follow him; the man at the door stopped me. Silently, almost grimly, he indicated a narrow cot at one end of the room. For a moment I hesitated, feeling the man's eyes upon me.

Sleep on my dead—I felt sure he was dead—friend's cot! Sleep in that fearful place! My whole being crawled with horror. I turned again to the man. His features were unyielding. Perhaps this was more third degree. Limp with weakness and weariness, I dragged my lagging feet towards the cot.

* * *

As long as I live I shall never forget my awakening. A uniformed figure, the chief, shaking me by the shoulder. Two other uniformed men silently watching. I sat up and gazed

81

about me, dazedly. Bright sunlight streamed through the windows. A stray gleam struck the cage. I shrank back, trembling. And yet I had slept soundly.

"Mr. Thornton," the chief said, "I have serious news for you. I have positive proof your friend is dead."

"Dear God!" The exclamation was wrung from me as recollection returned with a rush. "Where? You can't have!"

"Here." He thrust a bundle of letters into my hands. "You acted so strangely last night you caused me to suspect you of a serious crime. Also, you overlooked several important points. You got back from a trip only last night."

Last night! Surely it was years.

"You had left instructions to have your mail forwarded," the level voice went on. "These letters were evidently one day behind you. I picked them up at your rooms this morning. I took the liberty of opening them. Read this one." He selected it.

* * *

With trembling fingers I extracted from the envelope a single written page. I recognized the handwriting as the professor's. I read with feverish intensity, each single word burning itself into my consciousness:

Dear Thornton:

I am writing this in anticipation. I will see that it is mailed when my plans are completed. Too late, dear friend, for you to attempt, with the best intentions in the world, to frustrate them.

You will, perhaps, recall that many years ago, when I gave you my full confidence, I told you that I felt sure that the law of compensation would atone in some measure for my loss. Thornton, old friend, I believe that, in more ways than one, my hour has arrived. Two days ago I completed the absolute zero. But even better!

A man called here to-day. Although he did not recognize me, I saw through the veneer of added years with ease. Fate, call it what you will, my visitor is the man who wrecked my happiness.

Under pretext I shall detain him. I shall induce him to enter the crystalline cage. I have already arranged a dual control which the power will destroy when I apply it from *the inside of the cage.*

Please destroy the cage. It will have brought compensation to me before you read this.

Good-by, dear friend!
Wroxton.

"I apologize, Mr. Thornton." The chief offered a hand which I clutched in mingled sorrow and relief. The world had lost a genius. I had lost a dear friend. But he was right. It was compensation.

# RED CHURCH

by Dylan Henderson

THE AGING LANDLORD SEEMED SURPRISED TO SEE US when, shortly after two o'clock on August 1, 1978, we knocked on the door to his ground-floor office.

"I suppose I can show you the room," he said, scratching his bald head with a yellow fingernail. "You're really interested? No, no, that's good. I'm glad you want to see the room. Why not? It's not such a bad room. Sure, I can show it to you. Follow me. What were your names again?"

"Oliver Langdon. This is my wife, Gwen."

The old man wiped his palms on a greasy handkerchief and, smiling obsequiously, shook my hand.

"We don't get many new tenants," he said, as we followed him up the rickety stairs. "Most of the residents have been here … oh, at least twenty or thirty years. Joe Carrington—he moved into the Braxton about sixteen years ago. Most of the other tenants still consider him a newcomer."

I found the old man repulsive, but at the point in our lives, my wife and I had few options. We had spent what little money we had on our six-year-old son, who, due to a rare disease he had inherited from his mother, had spent most of his young life in a hospital bed. He had recovered—somewhat—but our family had accrued more debt than we could ever hope to pay. We had no choice but to sell our three-bedroom home in Park Hill and find cheaper lodgings in the city.

I paused at the top of the landing. Through the dusty window overlooking the yard, I could see a tiny, overgrown park, consisting of little more than a few elm trees and a swing set, wedged between a row of brick warehouses. To the southwest, not far from the river, the steeples of the Methodist, Presbyterian and Baptist churches towered over the shuttered factories and abandoned buildings that ringed downtown. Through the smog that hovered over that quarter, I thought I could see the grayish bulk of Mount Pocasset across the Watova and, crouching at the mountain's feet, the hazy outline of the Goodwill Refinery.

"It's not far from the downtown library," I said, trying to sound hopeful as I stared at the melancholy scene. "Alex will like that."

Gwen looked at me but said nothing.

"Your boy is a reader, is he?" the landlord asked as he flipped through the brass keys dangling from his belt. "Oh, he'll like the library. It's about six or seven blocks from here—on Kiowa, I think. It's a gorgeous building, you know. When I was a boy, I had a postcard with the dome on it."

The apartment he showed us was small, consisting of only five rooms. When the Braxton was built in the 1870s, he claimed, each apartment consisted of two large rooms: a bedroom and a drawing room, but tastes had changed, forcing the owners to remodel the old building after the war. As a result, the rooms were oddly proportioned, and the hallways unusually narrow. As for the kitchen, which contained a stove, an apron sink, an old-fashioned refrigerator, and a large table, it was not much larger than a closet.

The rent, however, was even lower than we had hoped, and in two weeks, Gwen, Alex, and I moved our remaining furniture, along with our books, clothes, and Alex's toys, into Room 304 of the Braxton Building.

* * *

On weekdays, I walked Alex to school and then took the bus to the local newspaper where I worked. One of my coworkers in the research department, a man named Tom Alsop, was surprised to hear that my wife and I had rented an apartment in what he called the Red Church District.

I had never heard that name before, and though I wanted to ask Tom about it, I didn't have the chance until the following Monday when Tom, the cartoonist Frank Tillmann, and I ate lunch together at the delicatessen across the street from the office.

"Where did you hear that name?" I asked, sitting down at the counter. "I've never heard it called that before. I thought the Braxton was in the Copper Dome District."

Tom, his mouth full, shook his head.

"No," he said, swallowing, "the Copper Dome District runs from Kaw to Muskogee. That's the southern boundary."

"I've never heard anyone call it that," I murmured. "I'm almost positive I've never seen that name in the *Herald*."

"How often does that part of the city appear in the paper?" Tom asked. "No one's interested in what happens south of Muskogee. It's a ghost town."

"Does your wife feel safe living there?" Frank asked, joining the conversation. "There's a lot of crime in that area, isn't there?"

I couldn't help but feel embarrassed.

"Not really," I said. "I mean, the neighborhood's all but empty. I never see anyone on the streets. The Braxton only has a few tenants—most of them elderly."

Tom didn't say anything. He was hunched over his sandwich, his elbows resting on the counter. Every now and then, he took a bite, which he chewed slowly and thoughtfully. He was an older man, closer to sixty than fifty, and one of the most knowledgeable in the office. I respected his opinion.

"Maybe there's not a lot of crime," he said finally, "but that doesn't mean you should feel safe."

"That seems paradoxical."

Tom smiled. His mood had changed.

"It probably is," he said, patting me on the shoulder. "Frank, that picture you're drawing is absolutely hideous. What is that thing supposed to be?"

\* \* \*

"Have you met our neighbor?" my wife asked later that week. "The one who lives across the hall in 303?"

I shook my head. I was sitting at my desk, staring at the trainyard across the river.

"He's a sculptor," she said, spitting out the last word as if it were foul.

"What's wrong with that?" I asked, somewhat amused. "It's an honest profession, isn't it?"

"I saw one of his … *sculptures* … when his door was open."

I looked up at Gwen. She seemed genuinely distraught.

"So? What was wrong with it?"

She sat down on the edge of the bed. Her hands were trembling.

"It was a thing—a pig—made out of clay. Only it wasn't really a pig. Its legs were too long—and thin. The whole thing was too lean...."

I turned my chair towards the bed.

"It does sound monstrous. Perhaps he isn't very good. He can't be when you think about it. If he were, he wouldn't live here, would he?"

Gwen tried to smile, but she still looked scared.

"He is good, though," she said quietly. "He's very good. Oh, it isn't just the sculpture, Oliver. It's this place ... this neighborhood. I don't like it. Alex doesn't like it either. It's too quiet. I never thought I would say that about a city, but it is. There are no cars at night. There's no one wandering the streets. I walked to the grocery store the other day—the little one at Eighth and Peoria. It was empty, Oliver. I didn't even see any employees."

It would be just like her, I thought, to make problems.

"Where do *you* suggest we go?" I asked, my voice rising. "Do you know of an apartment—anywhere in the city—cheaper than this one?"

Gwen's eyes were filling with tears.

"I'm not trying to fight with you, Oliver."

"It doesn't matter," I said, standing up. "It doesn't matter whether we fight or not. It doesn't matter whether this neighborhood is a slum or not. It doesn't even matter whether our neighbor is a decent sculptor ... or not. We can't afford to leave, Gwen. This isn't our home. It's our prison. We'll stay here until we're released."

"Just be sure you lock the door when you leave in the morning," she said, staring at a spot in the dingy carpet. "Will you do that for me?"

"I always do."

"Just be sure, okay?"

* * *

Frank Tillmann, the cartoonist, stopped by my office in the basement a few weeks later and asked me how I liked Red Church.

"It's okay, I suppose. My wife doesn't like it, but that doesn't surprise me. It's lonely out there, you know—or it would be if it weren't for the freight trains."

Frank laughed.

"You know, after our conversation that day, I asked Chris Morrison about the crime statistics for that part of the city. You were right, Oliver: they're lower than I thought. Did you know that, according to the census, less than two hundred people live south of Muskogee between Fourth and Ninth Street?"

I looked up from my work.

"That can't be right."

"Check the numbers."

Despite the heat, I felt suddenly cold, as if a gust of wintry air had swept through the stuffy basement.

"That's fifteen blocks," I said. "That's—what?—around twelve residents per block?"

Frank grinned.

"You know what happened, don't you? The church bought up all the property—the factories, the warehouses, everything. Morrison says the church even rents all the vacant apartments."

Frank must have seen by the look on my face how confused I was.

"You know, the old Catholic church—the Church of the Holy Rite—the Red Church."

"I don't know what you're talking about," I said, somewhat irritated. "The closest Catholic church is St. Patrick's on Apache."

"You are new to the city, aren't you? The main building burned down, Oliver, during the race riot. Only the rectory survived. A few years after the fire, some of the parishioners converted the rectory into a chapel. I guess a few of them still meet in the basement."

"The Red Church," I repeated softly, as if I were tasting the words. Even then, it struck me as an unlucky name for a church.

Frank watched me for a moment. Then, catching sight of someone in the hallway, he rapped his knuckles on the doorjamb and turned to leave.

"Tillmann," I called, rising from my desk, "wait a minute. Do you know how I can find it?"

* * *

One evening in late September, I had to work late, and I missed the last bus as a result. Downtown could be dangerous after dark, but the walk wasn't a long one, and I hoped to be home before nine.

It was a calm, clear night, but dark. The horned moon hanging over the freeway provided even less light than the dim—and often broken—streetlamps that lined the major thoroughfares. There were a number of men, most of them homeless, loitering outside of the library, but the streets were otherwise empty.

After a long and stressful day at work, I found myself relaxing. Since the move, Gwen had become increasingly difficult, and as much as I missed Alex, I was in no hurry to go home.

Instead of staying on Eighth Street, I decided to make a detour and turned west on Osage. A row of old factories, most of which had produced parts for the oil industry, lined the street. I stopped now and then to peer through a dusty window, but aside from rusting machinery, there was little to see. At the corner of Sixth and Osage, a cafeteria and an Italian restaurant, both of which had closed for the night, competed for the neighborhood's meager business, the rest of the street being comprised of warehouses, mills, and small shops that had shut down years ago.

The desolation that seemed to surround me on all sides began to affect my mood. I began to wish I had taken Tenth Street to Ottawa, thereby skirting this awful district. How, I wondered, could it be so empty? Aside from the electric hum of the streetlamps and the dreary sound of my own footsteps, the neighborhood was silent—unnaturally so. Every now and then, I heard a distant cicada wailing in one of the elms that lined Main Street, but that sad sound only depressed me further.

As I was crossing an alley not far from Fifth Street, I saw the Red Church for the first time. The brick rectory, all that remained of the original building, crouched between two much larger structures, which, though I couldn't see them in the dark, must have been warehouses or perhaps storefronts. Behind the rectory, a large square or courtyard, strewn with tile, brick, and bits of sparkling glass, marked the spot where the old church had stood.

Even moonlight could not impart luster to that dismal and melancholy scene. From what I could see of it, the rectory itself was a short, ugly building, the north side of its windowless bulk being covered in black mold.

And yet, something about the place intrigued me. Acting on impulse, I crossed the rubble-strewn courtyard and, circling the rectory, stumbled upon a dumpster behind the building. The thick, sweet smell emanating from within was almost overpowering. For some unknowable reason, a combination lock dangled from the lid, preventing anyone from so much as peeking inside the dumpster. After several vain attempts to guess the combination, I found I could lift the corner of the lid about an inch from the rim. Trying my best to ignore the stench billowing out of the opening, I jammed my flashlight into the opening and looked over the rim. Inside, there was but a single black trash bag, which, judging from the smell and the size of the bag, must have contained a cat or a small dog.

Something about the shape or outline of the bag unnerved me, but at that moment, I heard the door of the rectory swing open. Embarrassed, I switched off my flashlight and, cursing under my breath, crouched down behind the dumpster.

To my surprise, more than fifty or sixty people streamed out of the oddly shaped building. The alley was badly lit, the only light coming from a streetlamp on the other side of Osage, and my mind, colored by the place and the hour, imagined strange things. Some of the parishioners, being crippled by some malignant disease, shambled—or lurched—rather than walked. It seemed to me as if they kept to the shadows even more than the others. When I saw one of them in the moonlight, I almost gasped, for its baggy clothes could not disguise a hideously thin frame.

I hid for more than an hour, leaving long after the congregation had dispersed. What I had witnessed, pedestrian though it was, had alarmed me, and I dreaded meeting one of those strangely afflicted parishioners while traversing the shadowy streets of Red Church.

* * *

I expected my wife to be angry when I arrived home that night, but instead, I found her sitting on the kitchen floor, her legs shaking, her face as pale as a bedsheet. On the floor next to her was the revolver I had inherited from my grandfather.

"Are they still out there?" she asked, staring up at me with those haunted eyes of hers.

Without saying anything, I turned and left the room. I checked on Alex, who was asleep in his bed. Then I returned and, with a sigh, sat down at the kitchen table.

"If you want to indulge these sick fantasies of yours, then go ahead, but don't scare Alex with this nonsense."

"He's been asleep. He didn't see them."

"Who?"

Gwen swallowed. She was even more upset than I had realized. Unused to being alone at night, she must have tortured herself with the most ridiculous fancies.

"One of our neighbors—I think his name is John or Jim McDougall—came home about an hour ago. I recognized his voice. He has that, you know, really deep, gruff voice. He started talking to some of the other residents outside. I saw them through the window. Then—I don't know what happened— more people started showing up. There must have been fifteen or twenty people out there, Oliver. I heard…. I heard them mention your name."

At those words, all the warmth seemed to drain out of the kitchen, leaving behind an arid, bitter cold.

"I tried," she said feebly, motioning towards the kitchen window, "to watch them, but they saw me. One of the men picked up a rock and smashed the light over the front door. I … couldn't see anything after that."

I sat there, stunned, for more than a minute. Then I shook myself and, forcing down the panic rising within me, tried to think about the situation logically.

"I saw some people at the Red Church," I said slowly, trying to control the tremor in my voice. "McDougall must have been one of them. He … told the other residents that he had seen me there. That's all."

My wife was becoming hysterical.

"But why did they smash the light, Oliver? Why would they do that?"

"Some of his friends," I said, my confidence slowly returning, "are probably addicts, lowlifes, criminals—that sort. They must have seen you spying on them. They didn't appreciate it."

"Oliver," she said despairingly, "don't tell me you believe that."

"What other explanation is there?" I asked, leaning my back against the wall. I felt suddenly tired. It had been such a long day.

Gwen looked up at me. There were tears in her eyes.

"I thought they were going to … to rape me, Oliver," she blubbered. "I thought they were going to break in and … and … try to take me away."

I rose and, patting her gently on the head, picked up the revolver.

"Why," I asked, unloading the gun and stuffing the bullets into my pocket, "would anyone want to take you away, Gwen?"

* * *

Alex's first episode occurred in mid-October at De Soto Park, not far from the north bank of the Watova. It had been a warm day, and we had spent the afternoon walking along the river, watching the barges and occasionally fishing. Around two o'clock, Alex began to feel sick to his stomach, and while I waited for him near the railway bridge, he went behind a large cottonwood to vomit. A minute later, I heard him screaming.

Afraid of what might have happened, I rushed to him and found him pale and panting, his young face covered in sweat. No matter how much I tried, I couldn't get him to say what had frightened him.

* * *

"Did you notice," my wife asked, looking up from her magazine, "anyone in the lobby when you came home?"

I poured myself a glass of tea, refilled the ice tray, and sat down on the sofa. She was getting worse every day. Perhaps the disease she shared with our son had affected her mind.

"I saw Bill Galloway," I said, taking a sip of the tea. "He was arguing with the landlord about something."

Gwen, nodding to herself, turned the page of her magazine. It was as if she had forgotten I was there.

"Why do you ask?"

She looked up. Her eyes seemed strangely dull—almost lifeless.

"Haven't you noticed? There's always someone there."

* * *

That winter, Gwen's mental health continued to deteriorate. She claimed that, at night, she saw men-like things watching our apartment from the alley. During the day, she stayed indoors, too afraid to even leave the apartment. For a while, I would bring her books and magazines home from the library, but after a few weeks, she stopped reading them. Her other hobbies were soon abandoned. Even the blanket she had been quilting for Alex was stored away and quickly forgotten.

Shortly before Christmas, she became delusional and aggressive. She claimed that, not long after I went to work, a man—she recognized his unusually heavy tread—would climb the stairs and station himself outside our door. At times, she could hear him sniffing—and sometimes grunting—on the other side.

* * *

It was a rainy evening in January. Tom and I were standing at a bus stop in front of the Kearney Building, where we worked.

"I'm looking for another apartment," I said, shifting my umbrella to the other shoulder, "believe me. I'm looking through the papers every day. But it's pointless. The truth is we can't afford to move, Tom. Alex isn't doing well, you know. He keeps having these … episodes."

Tom nodded sympathetically but didn't say anything.

"Sometimes at night, he just … wakes up screaming. I don't know why. He can't tell us. Sometimes he hits himself. Sometimes he hits his head against the wall. It's like he's trying to wake himself up from sort of nightmare. I think … when he was sick … something happened to his brain. Maybe there was some sort of infection … or deterioration."

"Maybe there's something wrong with the apartment," Tom said, staring at the ripples at his feet. He spoke loudly, but even so, his voice was almost drowned out by the downpour. "There could be—I don't know—lead in the water."

"Maybe," I said listlessly. "The other residents…. Some of them seem to be sick, too. There's a man below us…. He has a … a sort of … odd face. His nose and mouth … stick out…."

A third person, an older woman, joined us, and I fell silent. Maybe I was losing my mind—just like Gwen ... and Alex.

The bus, running late, finally arrived, and the three of us boarded. The old woman sat up front near the driver. Tom and I chose a seat near the back. There were no other passengers at that hour.

"I'm going to have Gwen admitted," I said after the bus started moving. "There's a hospital in Lowake—I've been talking to the doctors there. I just don't trust her to watch Alex anymore."

Tom seemed surprised.

"Is that really necessary?"

"I don't know. She frightens him with her stories. Did you know that? Now he's afraid to ride the bus home from school. He thinks there are ... creatures waiting for him outside the building."

Tom was staring out the window. Despite the shine imparted by the rain, the landscape seemed dreary and sordid. To my mind, even Mount Pocasset, its dark slopes faintly visible in the light cast by the refinery, appeared strangely oppressive, as if its titanic bulk were a threat to everyone who lived in its shadow.

"I wouldn't want to live in Red Church," he said finally. "I don't know if you should or not. I'm surprised your landlord agreed to rent an apartment to an outsider, but—who knows?—maybe he needed the money. Maybe he thought the church wouldn't find out."

Tom must have seen the expression on my face and guessed—however faintly—how much I resented any support for Gwen's paranoid fantasies.

"I'm not saying," he continued cautiously, "that Gwen isn't ... hallucinating. She's obviously experienced some sort of breakdown. But I wouldn't be surprised if some of the parishioners were … taunting her. I doubt they like you living so close."

The bus was heading south on Ninth Street, having just passed Muskogee. The very district we were discussing was visible to our right, its brick warehouses and mills piled in a disorderly heap.

"It's just a normal church," I said defiantly. "It's like any other in this city."

Tom smiled. It was—no doubt—a good-natured smile, but at that moment, in the dim light pouring through the rain-streaked windows, he looked as if he were sneering at me.

"Have you ever gone there?" I asked. "In all the years you've lived in this city, have you ever attended a service there?"

"Never."

The bus, its pneumatic brakes screeching, rolled to a stop at the intersection of Ninth and Ottawa about a block and a half from the Braxton.

"Maybe I will," I said, standing up. "Maybe I will."

\* \* \*

By Sunday morning, there were four inches of snow on the ground. And yet, even beneath that blanket, the neighborhood still looked squalid. Repressing my misgivings, I kissed Alex and Gwen goodbye, locked the apartment from the outside, and then, shivering slightly in the cold, trudged down Ottawa to Fifth Street, which I followed north to the rectory the old folks referred to as Red Church.

As I approached that low, mold-stained building, a sense of apprehension began to grow inside of me. It was, for a church, a foul-looking place, its lot filled with thistles, trash, and weeds. Someone had dumped a pair of old mattresses, a broken table, and some chairs in front of the rectory, partially obscuring the times posted on the church's ancient sign.

Aware that the service might've already started, I walked quickly up the steps and, being somewhat nervous, yanked on the brass doorknob. The door didn't budge—it was locked.

I stood there for a moment, baffled. The snow-covered lot was covered in footprints. I could hear, moreover, though just barely, the sound of singing or chanting coming from inside the rectory. There was another sound, too, a rumbling sound, not unlike a pipe organ—though it didn't sound quite like any music I had ever heard, being completely devoid of melody. I tried the door again and then, laughing at my own nervousness, knocked on one of the oak panels. I knocked again—and the singing stopped.

Something about the silence that followed unnerved me. As silly as it sounds, I wanted to turn and flee from that miserable, rumor-haunted place as quickly as I could. If I had been less proud, I would have.

I must have waited about five minutes. No sound—of any kind—came from the church. It was perfectly still. I turned to leave, but as I was descending the stairs, I heard a sound. There were people behind the door. They were whispering.

I paused, uncertain what to do. Then the door swung open, and an old man appeared in the doorway. We stared at one another for a moment, and then, with a feeble wave, he motioned for me to step inside.

The interior of the rectory—or chapel—was all but bereft of furnishings. A pair of stiff-backed chairs and a dusty table stood beside the door. On the walls, which had not been repapered in half a century or more, a pair of crude tapestries, poorly made, depicted what I assumed were scenes from the New Testament. The only other object of interest was a Turkish carpet, worn thin by countless feet, which stretched from the foyer down the main hallway to an old-fashioned, five-panel door. The front of the house was not, as far as I could tell, *dirty*, but it had obviously not been cleaned recently or thoroughly. An unpleasant smell hung over everything, a noxious, unclean aroma, which reminded me of the poultry farms that lined the highway south of the city.

Obviously impatient, the old man clicked his tongue and motioned for me to follow him. As we passed a narrow door beneath the stairs, which must have led to either a closet or a basement, the smell suddenly waxed. For a moment, I felt faint and put my hand on the door to steady myself.

The old man almost screamed.

Shaken by his response, I withdrew my hand and, chastised, followed him to a room at the end of the hall.

Inside this small, low-ceilinged room, a dozen mismatched chairs had been assembled around an elaborate marble lectern. Behind the last row of chairs, in front of a bricked-up fireplace, sat two walnut pews, salvaged, I assumed, from the fire that had destroyed the church. I counted only six parishioners—all of them men.

Trying my best to smile, I sank into the nearest chair and, trembling slightly, turned to the podium. I tried to concentrate, but my mind had shut down. Everything ... everything around me had been staged. But why? I couldn't understand it. It didn't make any sense.

One of the men stood and, limping slightly, crossed the room to the podium. Like everyone I had seen in that awful place, he was old—and uncommonly ugly, his eyes being far too small for his wide, oddly proportioned face.

There was a book atop the podium. I could see from where I was sitting that it was too slim a volume to be the Bible—or even the New Testament. But the man treated it as if it were. He opened the book carefully and, licking his lips with his thick tongue, began to leaf through it.

I don't, truthfully, remember much of what he said. He spoke in a voice so low that I could barely hear the old man—even though he was standing no more than eight feet from where I sat. At times, he appeared to be reading from the book in front of him, but I wouldn't have been surprised to learn that he was improvising. The sermon, in any case, seemed unusually vague, consisting of little more than a series of disconnected generalities and shopworn platitudes. If the aging rector said nothing disagreeable, it was only because he said so little of substance. After about an hour, the service concluded with a brief prayer. Then the old man closed the book and, glancing in my direction, slipped it into the pocket of his jacket.

Outside, he shook my hand and said that he hoped I would return the following Sunday. His congregation, he said, was quite small and—no doubt—unimpressive, but their devotion was great, having weathered more challenges than most churches ever face. Though their resources were humble, they would do their best to make me feel comfortable.

I thanked him, and then I turned, walked slowly down the stairs, and crossed the snow-covered lot in front of the rectory. When I reached Fifth Street, I looked back at the Red Church, and when I saw that no one had followed me, I began to run. I ran as fast as I could, slowing down only when the dirty brick façade of the Braxton appeared on my right. The rector's hand— the hand I had held while looking into his tiny, piggish eyes— had been as big and as soft and as shapeless as a catcher's mitt.

* * *

102

The curator of the museum, a black man about fifty years old, worked in a small office overlooking the duck pond behind the building. When I introduced myself, he rose, shook my hand, and motioned for me to sit down in the chair across from his desk.

"Have a seat," he said pleasantly. "I understand you work for the *Evening Herald*?"

"I don't want to mislead you," I said, sitting down. "I'm not a reporter. But ... I would like to know more about the race riot."

The curator nodded slowly. He struck me as a serious, scholarly sort of man.

"There's been a lot published in recent years," he said diplomatically, "and the city library has a decent collection. Perhaps I can suggest a few volumes."

I wasn't quite sure how to proceed.

"Well ... I'm particularly interested in, uh, the Church of the Holy Rite. I understand it burned down during the riot."

"The rioters burned it down, sir—deliberately."

"Why?"

Mr. Gorham leaned back in his chair. I thought for a moment he might answer my question, but he just looked at me, his arms crossed over his chest.

"The riot," I said slowly, "as I understand it, began at the courthouse on Cherokee. From there, it spread north to Tuskahoma and then Aydelotte. But ... a contingent doubled back ... and set fire to the Church of the Holy Rite and a row of apartments on Osage. Why do that?"

The curator glanced at the open door, as if he were worried someone might overhear our conversation. When he spoke, he kept his voice low, his tone scholarly and detached.

"Most accounts," he began, "blame anti-Catholic sentiments. The rioters considered the community around the Holy Rite just as bad as the communities on the north side. In their minds, both were promoting degeneration, miscegenation ... degradation."

"But," I protested, leaning forward, "did the diocese even recognize the Church of the Holy Rite? I've talked to quite a few Catholics. Most of them said the Holy Rite was never, in any legitimate or orthodox sense, Roman Catholic. Even if it was, why didn't the rioters burn the cathedral on Apache? It was closer to the fighting than the Holy Rite was."

Mr. Gorham frowned. He looked displeased.

"Some people—old folks mostly—believe a lot of things about the Holy Rite. I've found that most people, if not probably educated, will always embrace whatever is most stimulating ... or titillating."

"The old folks—what sort of things do they believe?"

The curator sighed. Then he rose and, crossing the narrow room in just a few short steps, gently closed the door.

"It's an unpleasant subject," he said by way of explanation. "I don't want my staff to get the impression that I countenance what are, in effect, rumors of the crudest sort."

"No," I said, "of course not."

"During the first day of the riot, two of the instigators—Will and Ezra Harding—were killed, but their bodies weren't discovered until the next day. The man who found them claimed that ... the corpses ... had been mutilated—eaten. A rumor began to circulate—for whatever reason—that the Church of the Holy Rite, the Red Church, was responsible."

"The Red Church?" I asked, confused. "No one called it that at the time, though, right? I mean ... I thought it got its name from the fire...."

The curator smiled wanly and, pushing the door open, returned to his desk.

"No, sir, that's not true. Why, it's always been the Red Church."

* * *

After leaving the museum, I walked to the station on Cherokee and took a bus to De Soto Park, which runs along the Watova River and forms the southern border of the Red Church District. Retracing the steps Alex and I had taken that day, I followed the track along the north bank of the river for about a quarter of a mile until I reached the railway bridge. The old cottonwood was there—just as I remembered it. A faint aroma, barely perceptible, still clung to the area. Despite the fading light, it took me only a few minutes of searching to find the source lying beneath a pile of leaves. Something had been at it— a fox or coyote perhaps. The soft parts—the eyes, the nose, and the genitalia—had been eaten away. What was left had shrunk until it was little more than a dry, leathery bundle. It had been, at one time, a sort of baby, a runaway born in the tenements north of the park. It was unmistakably human—despite the long, thin arms, the teeth, and the snout.

* * *

I called home from the payphone at the corner of Fourth and Peoria, but no one answered. I tried again, and then I called Tom at the office.

"Will you check on Gwen and Alex?" I asked, barely able to control the panic rising within me. "I need you to go by the apartment."

Tom didn't respond immediately. I could hear him shuffling papers.

"Yeah," he said after a pause, "I can do that. What time is it now—about half past five? Okay, give me an hour. I'm almost finished."

"No, Tom, listen. You have to go now. You have to leave right now."

"Why?"

On the other side of the street, a man was watching me from inside a gas station. I had seen him earlier that day—at the park. He stared at me for a moment through the dirty window. Then he turned and disappeared into the shadowy interior of the building.

"I think … Gwen might be in danger," I said, holding the phone close to my mouth.

Tom sounded skeptical.

"Of what?"

I was almost hysterical. Why couldn't that goddamned fool just do what I asked?

"She might hurt herself," I said hurriedly. "I just talked to her on the phone. She said she was going to kill herself. She said … she said was going to kill Alex."

The connection was a bad one. I wasn't sure if Tom had heard me or not.

"Where are you, Oliver?"

Across the street, on the other side of Peoria, the door to a vacant building—a depot of some kind—swung open. A man wearing a baggy, oversized suit shambled through the dark portal, his face as expressionless as a mask.

"I'm at the southeast corner of Fourth and Peoria," I murmured, watching as the man, his gait truly bizarre, began to shuffle across the street, "but I … I might not be able to come home."

"Okay. Okay. I'll leave right away."

I hung up the phone. I was shaking all over.

The man with the wax-colored face had reached the sidewalk. He turned—or pivoted—towards me. Then with a sudden burst of speed, he lurched forward.

Everything that happened after that is a blur. I remember running down the alley behind the convenience store, my lungs burning as I dodged between the stacks of broken pallets stored behind the adjacent factory.

I could hear them now. There were at least three of them behind me. I could hear them calling to one another. And then, to my horror, I heard a cry—a sort of enraged squeal—rise above the general din. It was coming from Fifth Street, my only chance of escape.

Up ahead, not far from where the alley met the street, there was a row of casement windows, not much more than nine or ten inches high, near the roof of the factory. Desperate, I clambered atop a stack of rotten, splintered pallets, smashed the nearest window with my fist, and clearing away the glass with my elbow, began to crawl through the opening. On the other side of the wall, there was an eighteen-foot drop to the factory floor. Holding onto the window frame, my fingers already covered in blood, I lowered myself down as far as I could. Then I let go—and fell.

I lost consciousness for no more than a minute or two. A sense of danger revived me, and despite the pain in my feet, ankles, shins, and knees, I found that I could walk. There was a rusty staircase at the other end of the building, which led to an office overlooking the factory floor. Limping badly, I climbed the stairs and, finding the door to the office unlocked, stumbled inside.

A large round window occupied the middle of the room. I staggered over to it and, wiping away the thick layer of dust that coated the glass, looked out over Red Church.

Outside, beneath the darkening sky, the doors to numberless buildings, all of them supposedly abandoned, had been thrown open, and from within, a stream of dark shapes poured out, flooding the alleys, lots, and weedy, garbage-strewn courts that surrounded the Church of the Holy Rite.

At that moment, whatever hope I still had dissipated. I would never be allowed to reach the Braxton. I would never find my way home.

* * *

About three hours later, I pushed open the door to the Braxton, crossed the lobby, and limped up the stairs to the third floor. To avoid Red Church, I had walked all the way to Ingersoll on the other side of the Watova, using the bridges at De Soto Park and Tenth Street to cross and recross the river.

I leaned against the door for a moment, not even noticing the hole in the nearest panel, and then knocked twice.

Tom Alsop opened the door.

Inside, everything was as I had left it. There were no overturned chairs, no broken windows, no smashed plates or cups or bowls. I inspected every room, starting with the kitchen, and found nothing—aside from a tiny red spot, about the size of a fly, near the bathroom sink. I stood there for a long time, staring at that tiny spot. Then, trembling, I sat down on the edge of the bathtub, for I could not see to see.